# break

by

CD Reiss

ISBN: 1942833245
ISBN-13: 9781942833246

## chapter one

FIONA

Three words to describe the feeling of driving[1] with Deacon, trying to sit as if my ass hadn't just been ripped open. Vulnerable. Insecure. Guilty.

The paparazzi had been waiting outside the gates like fucking fuckers. Leeches. Slurping sucking animals who fucked you even when you said no. Who thought they were doing you a favor or at the very least thought they weren't hurting you when they were. They were.

Deacon hadn't said anything. He turned his face—blue eyes deadly, cheekbones of a god—toward one on the passenger side and stared down the man with the lens until he backed away from the car.

They knew who he was. A photojournalist. No more, no less. So they didn't know shit, but when he looked at people that way, they had to know he was a force of nature.

I put my fingertips on my cheek, slid them over to cover my mouth. My hand shook. How long had I been shaking? I hadn't even felt it. What parts of me were kinetic? I put my hand between my legs and hoped he didn't notice.

"I moved us out of Maundy," he said. "To the place in Laurel Canyon."

"What did you do with my stuff?"

"Your stuff is safe in your room."

I didn't actually care.

Who was I?

What was I supposed to do?

This wasn't new.

My ass hurt.

I was going to get Warren for this.

I'd said no.

One syllable and the same word in a dozen languages.

En-oh.

Deacon glanced at me. He was a dangerous man. If I told him about Warren, what would happen?

The easiest thing in the world. Like blowing up a building to take it down.

But they never talked about the mess it took months to clean up.

I'd said no. Clearly. And there I was with a ripped asshole while Warren was behind an electrified fence in a luxury institution.

The sun caught Deacon's eyes when he looked at me.

Never seen blue like that on a face. Not before him or since. Never seen a nose that had been broken so many times look so seamless. Nothing like it. And the look on his perfect face? Fuck him too. He couldn't tolerate lying, and I had to decide right then if I was going to do the intolerable.

Only Elliot had done things to me no man had before. He'd given me permission to choose to do things differently. He'd opened me the same way Deacon's look had, and Warren had walked right into the wound and ripped out my guts.

Deacon pulled up the private road off Laurel Canyon. I wanted to go home, and I didn't really have one anymore.

Why was I letting all these men do this to me? I was in the middle of nowhere, and I couldn't even get out of the car and get home. The door, the seats, the ceiling, and dashboard were leather-padded.

I laughed to myself.

Oh, God of irony, thou art great.

## chapter two

FIONA

Once we drove through the gate of the Laurel Canyon house, Deacon took my face and pulled me toward him. He kissed me in the way only Deacon did, owning me, sending a message that my mouth was his. I gave in to it, letting his tongue flick against mine, letting his lips guide mine in a dance of ownership. Even his hand was part of the kiss, pressing my jaw open. I breathed him in.

"Welcome back," he said.

Sex was never the point with Deacon. Sex was optional. Getting off didn't always mean unloading his balls on or in me, though when he did, I was in ecstasy. Getting off meant dominating me. And when I met him, it took me a while to understand that. Because I'm hot and horny, and he's a man. A man I wanted a lot.

But I'd forgotten a lot of things in Westonwood. And when I stepped onto the leaf-padded drive, I knew I'd changed.

And my insides hurt.

And I didn't know what to feel.

I was so confused. That caterpillar. Eating that leaf. And the pain. The same pain I'd felt a hundred times, but this time, I'd said no. I didn't ask for it. And that confused me and pissed me off, and I couldn't show it because Deacon's reaction wasn't something I could control.

The house was a classic, part of another small compound in the mountains. There would be coyotes, and he'd shoot them. There would be hippies and stoners, and he'd tolerate them.

Something about all of it made me sad. I should have felt relieved and safe, but all I felt was fucking sad. Not passive sad. Sad like I wanted to break something.

The house was furnished in hand-wrought chairs and wool rugs. I'd seen the place when he bought it, but I'd spent no time there.

"Where did you put me?" I asked before I could scream.

"Tell me what's wrong first."

We were headed into a conflict. We solved those by talking or by knotting. By me transferring my power to him. He'd ripped my memory from me in Westonwood without telling me what he was doing. Fucked me sane for half a minute. He'd do it again, and I wasn't sure if I could stand it. If he opened me, I didn't know if I'd be able to give myself time to think before he started making plans for Warren's destruction.

"I'm tired," I said. My guts were bubbling tar, foul and hot. Uncontainable. I wanted to destroy Warren. I wanted to do it myself, and I wanted Deacon to back the fuck up.

"You can tell me in bed." He took me by the shoulders. "Speak."

"It's stressful, that's all. Everything. What I did to you. And now I'm out, and I feel fucked up about it."

*And now you're a liar.*

*Use different words to describe yourself.*[2]

He didn't believe me.

We went into the house. He took off my jacket. I didn't have a thing to say. The house had windows like most houses had walls. He leaned on a chair and folded his arms. He had a leather band on his wrist, and a silver bracelet with a feather engraved on it. His hair was perfectly mussed, and his hands had built fences and dug ditches. They'd pulled triggers and tied ropes.

"Deacon, I..." Words failed me. They got in their own way.

He picked me up and carried me. I put my head on his shoulder.

"I'm sorry," I said.

"I know."

He laid me on his bed. It was still daytime, but I was stone-dead tired, lost at sea in the white foam of his duvet.

"Do you think our limits move? Did you ever think you would have let anyone hurt you like that before?" The words slipped out like escapees. I hadn't thought about them for a second, and there I was, watching them run into the field without looking back.

"Why do you ask?" he asked without reproach.

He was a picture in a magazine. Lit for his angles, the ruddiness of his skin, the light beard, the way his hair draped in a sideways S. Flawless and secure. A wish blown off a dry dandelion.

He brought his hand up and drew his thumb along my lips. Suddenly I wanted to open up to him. I wanted to be broken all over again. Now. Right there. I didn't want to wait until I'd put Warren in a box or wait until my ass healed. I wanted to crack like an egg for him.

And yet, I didn't want that at all. My intentions stabbed each other in the back.

"I don't know." Trying not to cry was the most obvious sign something was wrong, and I didn't want him to know. Not yet. So I didn't cry. I just knew my limits had shifted from a foggy line miles and miles away to a cinderblock wall I'd just been smashed against.

## chapter three

*TWO YEARS EARLIER*
FIONA

I leaned over Amanda and called into the little security mic on the driver's side. "Fiona Drazen."

The gate to Maundy Street [3] clicked and opened slowly, and the driveway lights flicked on. Amanda and I were sober. The handsome older guy in the leather jacket had specifically requested sobriety and more. We weren't permitted to even bring stuff with us.

"This better be good," Amanda said, turning her Mercedes into the gate. "Or I'm going to Phoebe's."

"There're a hundred paps outside that place. The rest are always pointing and looking away like they don't care. I'm sick of it already."

"You love it."

"You can take the car if you want to bolt," I replied, checking my face in the visor mirror.

"So you're staying the night? Jesus. You haven't even seen his dick."

"He's unbelievably sexy. I cannot deal with how wet I am right now."

She parked beside a Bentley, one of six or seven cars parked along the private street and hardly the most expensive. "Is this number two?"

I pointed at the steel number 2 bolted onto the front of the house. "I don't hear any music." I opened the car door.

"Maybe it's some old fart party."

We walked up to the door and rang the bell. A woman opened it almost immediately. She was in her mid-twenties, wearing a long silk dress that looked as if it were made of motor oil. Her figure was a perfect hourglass shape, and her posture made her seem taller than she actually was. Raven hair draped her shoulders, and her eyes were a clear blue that just looked clear in the night lights.

"Are you Miss Drazen?" Her voice was silky and lower than I'd thought it would be.

"Yes." We shook hands.

"And this must be Miss Westin."

"Hey," Amanda said, taking the woman's hand.

"I'm Tiffany. Come on in."

I glanced at Amanda. She touched her curls. She was so vain. She'd probably leave because Tiffany had better hair.

We followed Tiffany down the long, carpeted hallway. Her shoes were wicked high, explaining the height but not the posture, because they looked like they hurt to wear.

"Did Master Deacon explain what kind of party this is?"

"It's a kinky BDSM party," Amanda piped in. "Which is cool. I've been to those before. It's not a big deal."

I wished she'd shut up.

"It's a big deal to us," Tiffany said, stopping at a little wooden table in front of an interior door. "So we do ask that you sign non-disclosure agreements and liability waivers before entering."

She picked up two leather folders from the table and handed us each one. I opened mine and sifted through the paperwork. Amanda stood there with her folder unopened.

"It looks standard," I said.

My friend looked a little stricken. "Wait, what if something happens? We can't tell anyone?"

Amanda, at her core, was a worrier. The weight of every single thing that could happen kept her from doing much of anything, except when she drank or snorted or shot up. Then she didn't worry, and that was how she liked it. So taking her to a new place sober was already tricky.

"You don't have to participate your first time," Tiffany said. "As a matter of fact, we'd prefer you didn't."

"So then you don't need me to sign this." She handed back the folder.

"Amanda, stop being weird."

"I have a bad feeling."

Tiffany took the folder. "It's important that you be honest with yourself about your limits."

Limits. I knew mine. I had none.

"I'm honest about my limits." I signed the paper and snapped the folder closed. I handed it to Tiffany then turned to Amanda. "I'll find my way home."

chapter four.


FIONA

The room was flooded in sunlight, and still I slept. Deacon left and came back a few times. He crawled into bed with me and held me, stroked my hair while a headache raged through me. He gave me water, fed me. He took calls, and I heard him speaking Afrikaans in the other room, using a voice that had brought me to my knees a hundred times. I didn't realize how fucked up I was, how exhausted from Westonwood even before the events of the last day. But I wouldn't have slept for twenty-four solid hours if I wasn't.

In that haze of sleep, with all my filters down, I heard Elliot's buttercream voice.

*Count backward.*

*Use different words to describe yourself.*

*Fiona, listen*[4].

In my half-lucid state, I played the scene at the front door of Westonwood differently. I stopped. I listened to him. He said different things every time I rewound it and started again, but it always ended with him asking me to come home with him.

*Fiona, listen.*

When the fantasy ended well, I did go home with him, and I listened, and I slept until I woke biting back my scream, fogginess gone, too lucid, thoughts like broken glass.

I was alone in my new room, staring out the window at the little stables. I felt as if I were still in Westonwood, in a room someone else had made up for me. A box. A hole. The windows were open to the sounds of the wilderness, but I still felt imprisoned. The rustle of the leaves, the scamper of little night animals, the crickets. The dirt in my fingers. The twisting in my gut. Taking it like a whore, as I'd done a million times already except for the en-oh.

I couldn't sleep.

I didn't feel safe.

Warren was locked up, and I wasn't thinking about him. Or it. Or anything. I was trying to fucking sleep at two in the motherfucking morning.

I got up and walked down the hall. The light under Willem's door was on. I passed it and knocked lightly on Debbie's door.

She didn't answer. I walked in and snapped the door closed. She turned in the bed. "Fiona?"

"Yes." I crawled into her bed and put my arms around her. "You smell like soap."

I'd scrubbed myself red, drawing blood from my butt cheeks and twisting to scour the places on my back where he'd held me down. But I didn't mention it, because I was asleep before I was tempted to explain.

***

I woke from bed at dinnertime.

*Woke* being a word meaning, "bolted up straight."

*From bed* meaning, "Debbie's bed in a strange room Deacon owned."

*Dinnertime* meaning, "I was hungry, it was dark, and I didn't have a watch."

Outside, I saw the stables. They were the size of a school gym. The smell of horses had been painted over in studio white. The lights were on inside, and Deacon stood atop a ladder, stretching his mighty form to do something to the ceiling. He was shirtless, and from across the yard, his abs were tight enough to kiss.

I heard voices in another room.

A robe and slippers had been laid out for me. I put them on and followed the voices to the kitchen. I'd hoped to see Debbie, but from half a hallway away, I discovered Margie reading a file of some sort on the counter.

"Welcome back." She didn't look up from the file.

"Who were you talking to?" I asked.

"I'm really not sure." She closed the folder and turned to me.

I didn't realize my arms were folded across my chest until she looked at them, and as if her eyes were hands, she made them uncross.

"Come here," she said.

Belying her request, she came to me, three steps, *one two three*, and put her arms around me. Again, I had to fight the urge to cry.

"We all want to see you," she said into my ear.

"Not yet." I pulled away a little. "Just, can it wait?"

"I talked to Jonathan. He said you were acting strange when you left. And you looked beat up. Is there something you want to tell me?"

"Yes."

*Don't cry.*

*You wanted it, whore.*

*Use different words.*

"Okay?" Margie said.

The words were on my lips. *He pushed me down and raped me. He hurt me.* I was still hurt there. I could prove it. They could take pictures and do the kit. Though I'd washed away most of the evidence, I could talk about it. Then everyone would know, and they'd gossip, and it would be in all the papers, and the stink it created would be forgotten and…

"You want to tell me what?"

"Jonathan needs to worry about his own fucked-up ass."

She let me go. "Ain't that the truth." She snapped open her briefcase. "Do you want to talk business? Or Mom's spiraling nerves?"

"Business please."

"I'm glad you're back."

"That's not business."

"It is. But so is this. You're an outpatient, and you have to be under observation. Five sessions, just to make sure you're recovering. I got you the therapist you liked."

I almost breathed his first name, but stopped it in the tangle of longing and regret. "Doctor Chapman?"

I think I squeaked. I didn't want to see him because I wanted to see him so badly my ribs felt like jelly.

"Yeah. That's the one." She put the file in her case.

I felt pulled to the sky with joy and the earth with dread until the middle of me thinned and disappeared like taffy pulled to its breaking point.

"And your friend?" Margie added. "I think her name was Karen Hinnley?"

"Yes?"

"She's fine. Released this morning. Her lawyer called me and said she was asking for you. You all right?" Margie asked, snapping her briefcase shut.

"Hungry. I've been asleep for, like, thirty hours."

She slid her case off the counter and kissed my cheek tenderly. "Are you all right here? Do you want to come back with me?"

"I'm fine."

"Will you call me if you need anything?"

"No."

"Say yes."

"Yes. I promise. I'll call you if I need anything. Like a latte or a foot rub."

"Good girl." She started out the door but turned. "You can change, sister. Don't let anyone tell you that you can't."

"What if I told you I don't want to?"

"You're a shitty liar."

She walked out before I could prove what an excellent liar I was.

chapter five.

FIONA

Deacon had left my pager on the nightstand. It was his way of reaching me no matter what. My lifeline. My umbilical cord. I wrapped my fingers around it and checked it.

*—I'm in the stables—*

Out the door, to the left, in the stables. It would take me moments to get across that strip of yard. And then what?

I regretted getting into his car for the first time since I'd chosen it over Margie's. I'd needed to feel his protection— from myself and the world—at that moment, but I hadn't intended to go with him. I hadn't intended anything but to leave Westonwood, go to my place in Malibu, and not think about anything for a day or a year. I didn't delude myself into thinking that had been a good plan, but it was something. I felt derailed in that strange white house, with a man I'd tried to kill and no purpose at all except to hide what had happened in the hours before he picked me up.

And Elliot. I had to hide Elliot. He was mine. The memory of his fingers as they aligned the pen with the edge of his blotter, the lips that shaped his voice, they were mine. If I gave them life, my memories would be dismissed as a schoolgirl crush on a man who had helped me.

Now Margie, with the best of intentions, had requested him as my outpatient therapist. I was surprised he'd agreed. I knew he wanted me, and I knew the better part of himself would want to stay away from me.

Did he have a death wish for his career? Did he know how much I wanted to see him? How I looked forward to that first session?

I took a deep breath. I couldn't let Deacon see how excited I was about another man. He tolerated a lot of shit, but something about Elliot wouldn't sit well with him. And Elliot and I weren't going to happen. He was too good to be with me. He wouldn't let his dick lead him around. Not for long.

And I needed Deacon. I'd spin into crazy without him.

Shit.

I didn't know what I wanted. What a fuckup I was. What a royal fucking fuckup.

"Use different words to describe yourself."

"Excuse me?"

I didn't realize I'd spoken aloud until Deacon answered from the doorway.

"Oh, nothing. Hi," I said.

"Come with me." He held out his hand.

I did what I always did when he told me to do something. I followed instructions. I took his hand, and he led me outside. Crickets scraped their night song, and leaves and needles rustled in the shadows.

Deacon put his hand on the back of my neck and guided me toward the light of the bigger stables. "Maundy was going to have too many memories, so I thought we should start fresh."

He opened the side door, and light poured out.

The building had been converted into the party room, and a smaller extension into Deacon's private studio. It looked empty, without a table or a shelf, but the white cabinets built into two of the walls were obvious to me because I knew what was behind them.

"Have you used it yet?" I asked, looking at the thick hooks bolted to the crossbeams.

"I was waiting for you."

"I'm here."

"You're different," he said.

"That good or bad?"

He looked out the window, moonlight full on his face, glorious golden arms bent over his chest. He wasn't much of a talker, but he spoke with his lips and his hands.

"Get into position," he said. "I haven't changed that much."

Thank God. At least I knew what that was. I knew where it fit into the scheme of our relationship. I turned away from him and laid my arms together so that the tender insides of my forearms were pressed together.

A cabinet opened behind me, and he began.

chapter six.

DEACON

I didn't think this way until I walked out of Westonwood the first time, after you remembered what happened when you stabbed me. Before that, all I was worried about was whether or not you were sick. Or lonely. You don't like being alone, and I knew they had you in solitary for at least part of that stint.

I should have been relieved that you remembered.

But I wasn't.

There are things I've known about you from the minute we met. And I tried to power through. I regret that. There are horses you can train. Wild horses. The stallions you think will never have a rider. I've had two of those, and they'll only let me ride them, but they're not broken. They're not docile. Not really. Each and every one will turn on me if they can. Once you're wild, you're always wild.

You have no idea why you stabbed me, but I'm going to tell you.

You hate me. I'm an easy guy to hate. You're not alone. I get off on your pain. I get off on dominating you. You're small, and I'm in charge. Your goal is to please me, and that makes me feel good. I loved you because you hurt worse than any of the others. And now I know why.

Don't resist the ropes. They get tighter when you do. You know that. And don't argue when you model. I'm telling you this when you're knotted for a reason. Look at you, trying to shake your head. You'll rip your hair out to deny it. Stop it and listen.

Everything I've done to you goes against your nature. You don't fight it because you truly hate yourself. I can't cure that. Not with love or domination. So when you broke, you didn't really break. Not the way a real sub does. You got confirmation that you were right. I don't do that. I don't play with confusion. But I did, and it ends now. There are new rules. I'll take you and do what I want to you because you like it, but we have a new understanding, you and I.

You're not submissive, Fiona.

chapter seven.

FIONA

*I* *am so.*

*What the fuck are you talking about? We've been doing this for how long? You've been beating me raw, watching your friends fuck me, tying me into uncomfortable positions and showing me off. What the hell is that if not submissive?*

But I couldn't argue outside my head. I couldn't talk because he had a bit gag around my head, and my head pointing down at exactly the right angle to let my drool form a neat little puddle.

What the fuck was this?

*Deacon, you get in front of me where I can see you.*

*You let me talk.*

*You son of a bitch.*

*I hate you.*

He pushed me, and I swung, splayed like Peter Pan. I'd been glad he tied me with my clothes on so I could somehow hide what Warren had done to me, but now I didn't want to be tied at all. I wanted to run away. Somewhere.

"I love you, Kitten," he said. "And I'm sorry I tied you up to say this. But I need you to hear it, and I need your defenses down."

I screamed in my throat, but I couldn't move. This was such a shitty thing. The shittiest of shitty things. And again, in every way, I'd consented to it. I'd asked for this shit. Begged even. I couldn't be mad at him even though I was. He really thought he was doing what was best for me. And fuck him.

He kneeled in front of me so I could see him.

I said something through the gag that I hoped sounded like, "Fuck you." He pulled it down.

"Is this your shitty way of dumping me?" I spit out.

"See? Not submissive." He held up his finger. "You *enjoy* being sexually dominated. You only *require* someone else's control outside play, in the world. And this, I missed because I wanted you."

He didn't look half as upset as I felt. He looked like he always looked, as if he'd figured it all out and was just laying out the obvious.

"Get away from me," I said through my teeth.

"You're still mine." He was gentle enough to soothe, and firm enough to assure me.

"I don't know what that means right now."

"This is not my shitty way of dumping you. It's a way of redefining what we are."

"You need a sub."

He tsked and shook his head slightly. "I need to dominate, and I need you. But you don't *need* to submit sexually. Do you understand the difference?"

"I understand," I started as if I was agreeing, then I flipped it, "that the world is full of people telling me what I need and what I don't. You know what I need? I need someone else to get me down. I have to pee."

I didn't have to pee, but I wanted to be down, away, out of this room, and away from him and his fucking definitions. I already found Laurel Canyon oppressive, and the ropes around my body only reminded me of Westonwood strait jackets.

"Debbie can get you down," he said, standing. He kissed me on the mouth and strode out the door, his ass a perfect oval, stirring desire through my anger and confusion.

He closed the door behind him. Ten seconds later, it opened, and Debbie came in. She wore black jeans and a red shirt with three buttons undone. She was younger than me, but decades beyond me.

I must have been crying, because she took a red silk kerchief out of her pocket and wiped my cheeks.

"He hasn't been himself," she said.

She put her arms around me and held me as the ropes loosened and I fell. Debbie was my friend and more. She was a rock, a counselor. She put things in perspective even if I never listened to her. So I let her hold me, and she did it with affection and sincerity.

"I don't know what to do," I said.

"I have every confidence you'll figure it out. Be patient with yourself."

"Your hair smells nice."

"Willem is here," Debbie said.

"Ugh."

"He was a great help while Deacon was laid up."

Before I could articulate why I had to grunt at the sound of his name, Willem appeared. Deacon's younger brother was a solid muscular mass of what Dad would call distemper. I'd just call him a cranky asshole.

And as he stood in the doorway with his arms folded and a sour face from here to the LA River, my opinion wasn't changed. His hair was shorter than it had to be, as if he'd wanted to chop it off as an act of defiance. His eyes were as blue as Deacon's, but colder, sharper, scarier to everyone but the few of us who thought he needed an attitude adjustment.

"Hello, Willem."

His feet, in worn cowboy boots, were set far apart, knees locked, jeans rubbed-in with South African farm dirt. He got laid a lot because of his looks, but it was always a short-term thing.

"He might forgive you, but I don't," Willem said.

"Thanks for bringing that up. You can go home now."

Rather than go home, he strode in, heels clopping on the hardwood. His hair was lighter than Deacon's and his beard was a short growth of copper. "You bring shame on this family. You're dangerous. You can't control yourself. You're a child. A goddamn child."

Even without having been knotted ten minutes earlier, and even without Deacon having said terrible things to me and walking out, his words would have hurt me. I could tolerate being called a whore and a party animal. I didn't mind if someone called me stupid, but his thinking of me as a child hurt. Hurt bad.

"You're a bore, Willem. No wonder you can't keep a woman."

"That's enough," Debbie said in her Dominant voice. Willem wouldn't recognize the tone, but I did. "Will, Mary set out lunch for you. You should eat it."

I saw his conflicting emotions. He was compelled to obey, but he had more to say. He turned his body halfway to the door and looked at me as if he didn't want to lose so definitively.

"I don't deserve his forgiveness," I said. "I'll be around later if you want to yell at me more."

He huffed and walked out. We watched him go. Once he was out, Debbie and I cleaned up the ropes together.

I caught myself doing something weird. Something that tied together two parts of a disconnected story. I was walking the Laurel Canyon property, trying to do it straight so I didn't look like a rape victim, and as I looped the ropes into tight spirals, I had a fantasy.

In the fantasy, I told Elliot what Warren had done.

I told him straight and strong. I told him about my pain, physical and emotional. About where denying consent had gotten me. I told him I didn't feel like it was my fault. That I'd been clear. That I felt all right with myself about it. Fiona didn't blame Fiona. I blamed Warren and wanted to put my fist in his ass.

I fantasized that he understood. That he didn't get mad. He didn't try to wreak vengeance. He didn't act like a therapist, and he didn't act like a man on a mission. He took me in his arms and told me it was all right. That my reaction was normal. That my body would heal some day, but it would take time and I could be okay with that.

He kissed me in that fantasy, as he'd kissed me in so many. But I'd just been knotted, and my emotions were open and raw, and the effect of my imagination was sharp and strong. The hair on the back of my neck stood on end, and I froze, because I could taste him. My lips shaped themselves against his, and his want was real and deep, man to woman.

"Fiona?" Debbie said.

An idea was fixing in my brain, slowly with every fantasy, that it could happen. That he'd allow it. That I'd accept it. That I could be the adult Elliot had faith existed and not the fuckup Deacon accepted.

Debbie caught the ropes as they dropped from my hands. "What happened to you?"

I shook off the crust of Elliot, but not the core.

"I'm fine," I said, convincing myself I could muddle through. "Just fine. I have a shoot tomorrow with Irving Wittenstein. Can you imagine? It was scheduled six months ago, and I'm back just in time. It's crazy how things get back to normal. The machine keeps turning no matter what."

I smiled. She looked at me long and hard. She didn't believe me, and as much as I wasn't supposed to care what she thought, I realized I did care a great deal.

chapter eight.


*TWO YEARS EARLIER*
FIONA

Number Two Maundy stank of sex, and though there was low ambient music, I heard the cries and moans of people in pleasure and pain. Thwacks. Pops. The whoosh of a whip in the air and the hick of it meeting flesh. I'd done it all before, but there was something new about that night. I crossed my legs under the table and fidgeted with my soda, clicking the ice around until the edges were gone.

My friend Ahmed and I had gone to the Dome in New York a few times. We'd rented a couch and a Mistress had led a girl to me on a leash. She'd knelt before me, and I opened my legs to her. I called her a good little bitch when she licked my cunt, and I came good and hard. But I'd felt like a visitor even after the Mistress kissed me on the mouth.

I didn't feel like an observer on Maundy. I wasn't looking in the window. I wasn't an honored guest but a piece in a puzzle. I only had to be snapped into place.

In front of me, across a narrow marble strip, crouched a naked woman on all fours. Her hair was tied in a neat bun, and her back was planar under the weight of a man's feet as he reclined on the grey couch. She didn't move, even when the sole of one shoe pushed on her, leveraging against her as if she were a coffee table.

He put his iced drink between her shoulder blades. No coaster. She winced from the cold but didn't even look as he turned to the second woman kneeling before him. She wore garters and had pink hair and tattoos.

He put his finger down Pink Hair's throat. She took it. All the way down. He thrust his finger into her repeatedly, fucking her mouth with his hand. He wore a suit, but he wasn't Deacon.

*Master* Deacon Tiffany had called him. Suited him. I wasn't surprised.

I sat alone, riveted by the coffee-table woman. Tiffany had walked away seconds ago, after walking me through and seating me. I'd seen all the trappings before: the straps in the walls, the hooks in the ceilings, the wooden Xs between the windows that overlooked Los Angeles.

"What do you see?"

I spun around to see Deacon standing by my side. I'd only seen him sitting in the front seat of his car. He was gorgeous when he stood. Tall. Straight. Shoulders in a dark suit tapering to a slim waist. Shirt open a few buttons. Tooled leather belt with a buckle shaped into two twisted feathers.

"A lot."

"May I sit?"

"It's your party."

He sat. To my left, someone came with a grunt and a cry. I couldn't even look, he was so gorgeous. So self-assured. He had confidence where most men had no more than their cocks.

"I don't usually come downstairs, but Tiffany said you were here. She said you came with a friend."

"She left."

He nodded. The light from the little table lamp brought out the hard precision of his face. The short beard, the scar on his cheek, the one on his beautiful upper lip. His tongue flicked out, licking his lip so quickly I barely remembered it happening. "What do you do, Miss Drazen?"

"Like, for a living?"

"If you want to call it that."

I shrugged. "I'm seen. I get paid to wear things people want me to wear. Or get photographed. Otherwise I have plenty to live off."

"Who photographs you?"

"I have something with Irving Wittenstein on Wednesday."

"Impressive."

"Not really. I just go and smile. Look defiant. La-di-da."

"You make people think of you for a living. You remind them you exist."

I hadn't ever thought of it like that, but something about it made me bristle. "I don't care what they think."

"I'm sure you don't."

He didn't believe me. I could see it on his superior grin. He'd believe it soon enough.

"What do you do?" I asked. "Just the club?"

"I'm a photographer." He'd only lied a little. He didn't know me well enough to tell me what he really did.

We smiled at each other then. Stupid thing. To find a connection between his job and mine. I met Hollywood people all the time and had more in common with them than I had with him, but I felt something click nonetheless.

"You're watching this scene play out," he said, pointing across the marble path.

Another man had joined the scene, kneeling in front of the coffee-table woman and unzipping his pants. He was in his twenties, handsome, tattooed—what hipsters tried to be when hipsters tried to be rough.

"Yes." I didn't have more words, because the rough man put his cock in her mouth and pumped, looking elsewhere, and she couldn't rock with him. Couldn't spill the cold drink. I was a throbbing gushing mess, watching him fuck her face. My clit was a hard nodule, and I pressed my thighs together because it felt good.

"What about it appeals to you? Or disgusts you? What intrigues you?"

"That's a personal question."

"It is, but you've got your legs crossed for a reason. I bet if I put my hands between them, like this"—he slipped his hand over my knee to uncross my legs and drew his palm up the inside of my thigh—"you'd open your legs."

Under the table, my knees parted for him. He went under my skirt. I was on fire, and I was a whore, generally, so letting a strange man finger me was just another Tuesday.

Except it wasn't, because no one had ever touched me like they owned me. No trepidation. No questions. No fumbling. Just his thumb along the line of my underwear.

"This scene," he said. "He's fucking her face, and it's doing something to you. When I touch you, you're going to be wet, and your clit is going to be hard. Your lips will be swollen, and you're going to come in only a few strokes."

He had a point. No reason to be coy. Fuck it anyway. I was above people's judgments.

I ripped my eyes from the scene and put my elbows on the table. I wasn't ashamed of feeling the way I did, and I wanted to be utterly clear with him about that. "Make me come, then."

"What turns you on, Kitten? What about the coffee table?"

"He's using her. I see the scene, and I'm turned on. She's not even a whore. She's insignificant. Nothing. Unworthy of anyone even looking at her. Not even worth degrading…and I want it. I want it now."

"It takes time to get there, Miss Drazen." He spoke as if his hands weren't teasing my skin.

"Time is one thing I have plenty of," I said. "And money."

He pressed his lips together and looked me up and down. "I don't need money." He seemed genuinely interested and detached at the same time.

His thumb brushed my clit.

"Oh—"

"Shh. Look at me. Act as if nothing is happening under the table." He put his fingers on the walls of my opening. "Do you imagine you're her, or the man with his dick in her mouth?"

I obeyed him, trying to look as if this was dinner conversation, but there was no tablecloth. Anyone who looked could see his hand under my skirt. "I am her."

His finger brushed my clit.

"Watch her."

I turned from him as he stroked the length of my wetness so gently. The rugged man pumped the naked woman's mouth as if she were a hole in the wall.

"She's not even moving," Deacon said. "Not even sucking his cock. She's a receptacle. She has no will of her own but to please him."

He pulled out and shot streams all over her. She left her mouth open, but it was obvious he wasn't interested in keeping it neat. He came in her mouth, on her cheeks, her eyes. He left her with her mouth open, come dripping off her face, not wiping it away or looking at her as he tucked himself back in. It was so dirty and degrading, especially when he stood and zipped his fly as if she wasn't even there. She couldn't wipe it away. She just dribbled like an object.

The man in the suit dropped a wadded up napkin on her back. It was that act and the Master's fingers on my clit that brought me to orgasm.

"Look at me," Deacon growled.

My face contorted and my muscles tightened, yet I stayed still as his fingers stroked my clit, and I came and came. Eye to eye. He was so powerful, and I was under him. I'd known him a few minutes, and already I was a servant in his kingdom.

# chapter nine.

FIONA

I checked my watch. I could make it to my appointment with Elliot before Irving. Just get it done with. He was across town from the photographer's studio, but I could do it. Just take the 10 to Robertson. Go north.

Deacon had made sure my Bentley was waiting for me at Laurel Canyon. Complete tune-up. Full tank of gas, new wiper blades.

North to Wilshire.

Over to Westwood.

Wait. Right or left?

You'd think I hadn't lived here my whole life.

I should have used a driver. I wasn't functioning right. I was disoriented in my own head, never mind the west side.

I found Elliot's office just north of Santa Monica. A pleasant non-descript building with industrial carpet and hardy plants in pots. The whole building buzzed with therapists and clinical social workers in private pods like a hive of encouragement.

I checked my watch outside his door. I had plenty of time to get to Irving, but I was as eager to skip my appointment as I was to make it, and a shoot with Irving was the perfect excuse.

Elliot opened the door clothed in professionalism.

What a handsome little fucker. He looked at me from toes to eyes, and I turned to liquid. Not fire. Just a melted mass of tears and emotions. A sort of surrender I hadn't experienced.

I wanted to run toward him and away from him at the same time.

chapter ten.

ELLIOT

I took outpatients once a week in an office in Century City. It was small, and clean, and on the impersonal side. My office in Westonwood had more of my touches, but I was there twice a week, and the patients there would be put off by a standard, sterile therapy room.

I rearranged my desk, dusted a shelf that was already clean, and considered meeting her out on the patio. I hadn't wanted to be her outpatient administrator, but once her sister/lawyer requested it, saying no wouldn't have looked any better than saying yes. I still held out hope that this would all go away. She'd walk in and seeing her out in the real world would kill my feelings.

"I don't think that's in the cards," I said to the brass cross on the back of the door.

My mother had given it to me when I'd taken my First Communion. The dying Jesus was symbolized by a flat, stylized shroud. No tortured three-dimensional body like a Catholic crucifix. Just a symbol of death and resurrection. I'd prayed to it a hundred times. It never answered, but it wasn't supposed to. The conversation was with myself.

"I think I should just sign off on her. Just say she's fine and let her go. I don't…I don't understand what's happening to me. I love Jana. She's good for me. A hundred times over, she made sense. And thank you. Thank you for her. But I'm throwing her back in your face. You set me up, and I reject you. Or not."

*Tell me something.*

*Tell me how I'm supposed to discern what to do?*

*She's going to walk in here in a few minutes, and I'm going to what? Tell her how I feel? Lee is right. That's a massive breach of trust. I don't know if I can even sit through the five sessions with her. Five sessions. That's all I have to last. The length of her outpatient probation. Then I cut her out of my heart. I have to do that. I have to guide her through the transition and move on. I need your help, God. Jesus. Holy Spirit, listen. Just give me the strength. Back me up here. Do what you're supposed to do.*

I wasn't entitled to pray for God to do his job, because it wasn't his job to make things easy for me. But I needed help, and when the little light went on telling me that there was a patient in the waiting room, my heart jumped.

*Maybe I'll open the door and I won't care.*

*Maybe I just needed to leave Jana to change.*

*Maybe she'll be just another patient.*

I opened the door.

Her feet were pressed together, and her bag was in front of her. I was a dead man. She didn't look particularly beautiful. She hadn't made herself up. Hadn't dressed to the nines, or any other number, but something about the color of her skin and the way the sun through the window hit the ends of her hair just clicked with my desire.

"Come in." I stood to the side and let her in.

"No couch," she said, surveying the room. "How are you going to hypnotize me?"

"I'll get one in if we need it."

She sat. I sat. My desk faced the wall, so I turned the chair around. There was nothing between us. I could smell her perfume.

Her foot pointed and straightened. Her naked flexing ankle. My lips around the bone, popping off, letting the tongue linger.

"How are you doing?" I asked.

She pressed her lips together as if she was keeping them from saying what was on her mind.

"You can tell me."

This was a breach. Posing as a therapist so she could tell me what was wrong when I would use all that to bring her closer to me.

She looked down.

Her recalcitrance wound me tightly around the spool of concern. When she pinched the bridge of her nose, I had to grip the arms of the chair to keep from kneeling before her.

"It's nothing," she said.

Needless to say, my glands fired. Nothing didn't mean nothing. Nothing meant "I'm not telling you," and knowing there was something wrong that she wouldn't share, that I couldn't help her with, or protect her from, made my skin prickle with angry heat.

"Fiona." I growled it in the most untherapeutic way imaginable.

Shit. I'd crossed the line.

"I can't do this," she said, standing.

"Wait—"

She headed for the door, and I got between her and it. Her chest heaved, and her eyes looked panicked.

"You have to know," I said with my hands up, "I'd never do anything to hurt you."

"I know."

*Do not fuck this up by thinking with your dick. She needs you.*

"I'm here for you. Not the other way around. If you want to talk, this is the place to do it."

She crossed her arms and took a second to realign her jaw. As strong as she tried to look, she was falling apart at the seams.

"You want to talk about something?" she said.

"Yes."

"You want to talk about something really painful and hard?"

My hands landed on her shoulders as if they had a will of their own. God damn my porous boundaries. "Talk to me."

"I want to tell you things I won't tell anyone, but I can't. You'll just make me relive it, and you'll want to tell people who will only make it worse. But you have this way…you open me up. You crack me open and pour me out, and all you do is look at me. So you need to stop looking at me because it just makes me love you more."

Her eyes went wide with shock, as if she'd just been slapped or surprised by what she'd said. I took my hands off her shoulders, because I didn't want her to feel pressured, but she took it as a sign to leave.

I let her go, because that was the professional thing to do, and as I stood there looking at the seam between the door and jamb, my father's voice broke the fog of my disbelief.

*Go get her, you stupid shit.*

## chapter eleven

FIONA

Elliot burst out of the building just as I was opening the car door.

"Wait!" he called.

I didn't. Because fuck everyone. And my brain. Fuck my brain and my stupid mouth. I must have been out of my motherfucking mind.

I didn't love him. I loved Deacon, who was perfect for me, even if I wasn't submissive according to him, and who I still wasn't sure about, love or no love. All these men. All of them could go fuck themselves.

I peeled out of the parking lot, leaving that fucker in the rearview. He'd almost gotten to me. Almost made me tell him about Warren. Well, I wasn't ready. That shit at the creek did not happen, and I was not recounting it for him, and I didn't love him so fuck my stupid brain.

*Use different words.*
*Confused brain.*
*Truthful brain.*
*Lying, stupid brain fuck the holes in my brain.*

Of course, there was an accident on the 10. The 10 was an accident factory.

"Late!" I said to the dashboard. "That's a word I'd use to describe myself. Late."

I wasn't late. Not yet. But I needed to call myself terrible things.

"Late," I said, speeding across Santa Monica Boulevard. "Of course there's traffic, and I'm late."

I focused on getting downtown without killing myself or anyone else. My hands loosened, my breathing slowed, and I got there in one piece. I checked myself in the rearview. I couldn't even see myself. I looked like a Fiona Drazen mask.

Fuck it. I took a deep breath and got out of the car.

Irving Wittenstein was the best celebrity photographer in Hollywood. He had been when we met, the Wednesday after Deacon put his fingers up my skirt, and when I got out of Westonwood, he was still the best. Worthy of keeping a six-month-old appointment at the worst time in my life.

He had a studio in the guts of downtown between a garment factory and a Mexican food warehouse.

"Hey," I said when he opened the door.

He kissed both of my cheeks. "Welcome back."

He was a clean-cut guy with a serious face and an arm that had lost the battle with polio when he was a child. But he managed to come off as handsome and competent, and when he'd taken my picture the first time, I looked at the results and felt as though the camera saw my insides.

Which, at the time, had seemed like a good thing. Back when I was young and stupid, or just stupid. Before Westonwood, and days before Deacon got me under control.

Before Warren.

Which I realized I was trying not to think about. I told myself I was all right with it, but if I was all right with it, I wouldn't be thinking about it all the goddamned time.

"You look rested," Irving said at his door. "Your team's here."

My team. Right. I had a hair stylist. A makeup stylist. A makeup applicator. A clothing stylist. A nail person. Each of them had an assistant.

*Look casual.*

I smiled and put my hand on his lame arm. "Wanna do something real?"

"For *Vanity Fair*? Not likely."

I didn't think I was sabotaging the shoot. I thought of it as bringing it to the next level. No more same old, same old. I walked into the green room and was immediately attacked by giggles and kisses. Someone put a drink in my hand. I heard the words "blow" and "flake" in the form of a question.

"Stop!" I said, throwing up my hands. I put down the drink.

They had huge kohl-lined eyes and open red lips.

"I'm doing this different. You'll get paid. But get out." I pointed toward the door.

"Come back for the next shoot."

They hustled out until it was just me, Irving, and Piper Lundgren, the *Vanity Fair* editor. With a crop of bright white hair and a soft blue jacket by a Japanese designer, she looked like an ad for New York City.

Once the last of them went, Piper slow-clapped. "Stunning performance."

I kissed her cheek then the other.

"So wearing Photoshop then?" she asked.

"Oh, shut up." I powdered my nose. I'd do foundation, mascara, lipstick. No more than that. "Let's make history again."

"You getting naked again?" she asked, brow raised.

I hadn't known what I wanted out of the first shoot, but I hadn't thought about making history or anything else.

The last cover I'd done for *Vanity Fair* had excited and scared the shit out of me. I'd been naked but for shoes and a copy of *First Touch* covering what couldn't be printed. The book itself was about a woman understanding her need to be dominated and degraded, a journey I was about to begin during that first shoot, and a journey that was about to end during the second.

That first shoot had taken on a life of its own, and when I wiggled into the silken drapey thing I was supposed to wear and the air-light fabric touched my skin, I shivered.

Deacon had been at the first shoot.

A man I barely knew.

He'd shown up because he knew Irving, and I'd asked him to stay. Irving had it under control, but Deacon distracted me with the burn of his gaze.

"If you're going to undress me with your eyes," I'd said to him in a room full of people, "why not just ask me to get undressed?"

The room went silent. Someone turned off the music. Piper bit the end of her pencil and looked at Deacon as if she wanted to jump his bones, but he kept his focus on me.

With half a smile, he said, "Take off your clothes."

It wasn't salacious. It wasn't "Show me your tits," which I'd done a hundred times, even sober. It was uttered in a normal tone, and it was an order.

I unbuttoned my shirt, and the reaction from the stylists and friends was hooting and howling with a side of clapping. Piper looked unsure. Deacon's eyes didn't move off me.

"Out!" Irving shouted, waving his good arm with the camera at the end.

I kept unbuttoning, because outside Deacon and me, no one was in that room. And Irving, doing his fucking job like a fucking badass, took those pictures. I'd been cut open, turned on, high on little black pills and the man with the blue eyes.

Deacon had been the one to pick up *First Touch* off a bench and hand it to me to cover myself. I got on my knees and opened my mouth. Spreading my knees on the floor and putting the book between my legs. Forearm over my little breasts.

The book was a reflection of how I felt, and how I wanted to feel. How I looked. Like a degraded slut with a ton of money.

The cover had been famous, and if the paparazzi couldn't get enough of me before, the nude added to their hunger.

I hadn't intended to go on without makeup when I got the booking for the second shoot. Piper flipped open her phone, and Irving relieved her of it. He was great. After Westonwood, he was the only one I trusted to photograph me.

I shouldn't have trusted anyone.

I should have stayed home, wherever that was. Crawled into my dusty condo on Venice Beach and stretched out in the middle of the floor. Let the sun set on me, keeping all my shit in the dark. Because the dark was where it all belonged. Deacon. Warren. Elliot. Debbie. Even Willem, who annoyed the holy fuck out of me.

But the lights, and the heat, and feeling all those people looking at me…

"You all right, Fiona?" Irving said, camera down. He changed the roll of film. "I was going to do some large format stuff, but if you don't feel it…"

"We can't reschedule," Piper said.

"I feel it," I said. "I'm fine."

Because fuck Piper Lundgren from *Vanity Fair*. I could turn this shit on and off in a heartbeat. This was my job, mother-fucker. This was all I had to do. Party, be seen partying, get photographed between parties.

"I'm putting a strobe in and using slower film," he said, snapping the large format cartridge into the camera. "So no quick moves." He put the camera on a tripod.

"Okay." I nodded more to myself than him.

"Fiona?"

"Irving?"

"Are you all right?"

"Do you want me to repeat my safe word? Or are you just going to believe me?"

Party.

Be seen partying.

Get photographed between parties.

I looked at the camera and jutted my hip to the right.

"Open up, Fiona," Irving said.

The flash went off, and I was exposed. Bare. Skin and mask ripped away. All defenses burned to the ground. It wasn't the flash. It was the flash and time. The lens found the cracks. It was him telling me to open up the millisecond before I couldn't shore myself up, and the flash going off, and Piper with her bitten pencil, and the four-thousand-dollar dress, and Deacon's voice when he said he wasn't going to break me, and that god-fucking caterpillar in my face as I was a little shit-eating whore with an asshole surrounded by sentient skin, and I choked.

I just choked.

I choked on spit and bile, and both came out in a sob. A part of me was thinking, looking at myself, observing the melt-down with crystal clarity, and saying, "Oh well, I guess we're doing this now, are we?"

And I did it. I dropped to my knees and wailed. Every ounce of pain came though my face. My narcissism and self-loathing. My moral emptiness and emotional fullness. I wasn't prepared for pain. Wasn't raised for it. And it hurt. Everything hurt. I felt so alone, so abandoned, so worthless, and at the same time so cherished and prized, burdened with a responsibility to strangers I couldn't shoulder. Not through what I'd done. Not through hurting Deacon. Not through this grinding foul hate I couldn't ignore.

I didn't know what I was saying as I twisted my body on itself and wept. Large-format abandoned, the camera clicked even when I got back up on my knees and looked into my cupped hands, where I'd caught a line of spit. I thought how much they looked like leaves, and how the streak of mascara across my palm looked like a caterpillar. And I got mad.

I'd gotten away with everything in my life. I'd banged up cars, spent money, done more drugs than a body should be able to do. And Warren was from my tribe. He'd walk away. I knew it was the truth. The only one who could punish him for what he'd done was me.

I looked at the ceiling and cried out, because I was joyful in my rage. My face was smeared with kohl. A red gash of lipstick lacerated across my cheek. The dress had shifted, exposing a breast.

They'd ask me later if I'd been aware of the camera. And I was. Of course I was. I was born to be aware of the camera. But I was also born to be honest before it.

I was born to party.

To be seen partying.

To be photographed between parties.

And there was my power.

This life was my life. Fuck anyone who tried to take it away.

## chapter twelve

FIONA

I left the studio drained. Nice and empty. I was going to spend the night filling myself up with something fun, something positive for a change. I was done with this weepy shit. My life. My choices. My control.

As if he'd heard my determination, Deacon was leaning on my car when I got out of Irving's.

When he saw me, he opened the passenger side for me. He'd taken the fucking liberty of putting Wagner in the stereo.

I approached him, eyes locked on his, his face peaceful and powerful, as if I was just a section in an orchestra he conducted.

"I don't do this old world shit," I said.

"You fuck to it all the time."

I swallowed. I'd done lots of things to classical music, mostly staying still while being manhandled, and they all flashed through my head. "Who said anything about fucking?"

See, that was a denial. I was telling him I didn't want to fuck him, even though I did. And that meant I was looking for a sweet beating or a knotting or something else. But I wasn't looking for anything I would have looked for before. I didn't know what I wanted besides swift, sharp change.

He saw that. In the way he looked down, and the way his sculpted hand moved a lock of my hair away from my eyes, he saw everything. "What's going on with you, Kitten?"

"You're the one who jacked my car."

"Get in then." He stepped aside, and I got in the passenger seat. He slapped the door closed and walked around the front. Jeans. Boots. Jacket. Six-three in a full suit of badass.

"Where are we going?" I asked.

"Where were you headed?"

I had been headed somewhere he wouldn't want to go. Somewhere he wouldn't be welcome, where he'd see things he didn't want to see.

"Is this what you meant by 'not submissive?' You my chauffeur now?"

"I'm whatever you need."

"Let's hit the 405." I snapped the lap belt closed. "Really open this bitch up."

"I can't get arrested."

"I know."

Deacon was on a watch list. He could move in and out of the country, but if he was arrested, the domino effect from the investigation would put him in jail, or worse, get him extradited to Sudan. He'd never elaborated on why that was bad or what he'd been caught doing in Sudan, but I had enough of an imagination to make me not ask.

"I'm moving out," I said. "I'm going back to my place in Malibu."

I saw him mostly in silhouette against the painted sunset and grey geometry of the city. He looked like he wasn't going to answer, but I knew better. He didn't speak for the sake of speaking or answer because I'd asked a question. He was a Dominant, a Master, and he knew his words had power.

"I need to know you're all right, and when you're not living under my roof, anything can happen. That's very uncomfortable for me."

Saying it was uncomfortable for him as well, that I knew. He didn't enjoy expressing his feelings as much as he enjoyed acting on them.

"I'm sorry," I said. "I don't know if I can be that for you anymore. You said so yourself."

"You'll always be mine, whether you're submissive or not. You can just make it easy or hard."

"I don't want it to be hard for you, but something changed. I don't know what changed. Believe me, I'd love to have things stay the way they were. I never felt so safe as with you on Maundy. But it's not the same. And I don't mean the location is different. I mean…something happened in Westonwood."

I froze. I meant something psychological. I meant a change in my own chemistry. But to my ears, it sounded like I was segueing into Warren.

"With the doctor?"

"No!" The denial came too hard and too fast. "Yes, but no."

We hit the 405, and I thought for the first time that maybe he shouldn't open this bitch up. Maybe he should drive straight and clean and well under the speed limit.

"Yes, but no? What does that mean?"

"Are you jealous?" It was a ridiculous question. Deacon wasn't jealous. He just didn't have that gene.

"Just tell me," he growled. "I want to know."

Yet he'd avoided my question.

"Yes, he changed me, because he asked questions and told me things and saw me in a way I've never been seen before. But to the heart of what you want to know, no, I didn't fuck him."

The acceleration of the car was so smooth and powerful, it reminded me of a horse moving fluidly from walk to canter to gallop. And Deacon, whose grace always reminded me of a stallion, was wound tight.

"I don't care if you fuck him!"

I'd never heard him raise his voice. Ever. I didn't know if I looked as deer-in-headlights as I felt.

The car sped into the eighties. The freeway was empty for a change. The *whup* of the tires under me was soothing. I paced my breathing with the seams in the road.

"Deacon. I was joking. Slow down!"

"You let him in!" His hair whipped over his forehead, and mine swirled over my face.

"He was my therapist."

"He loves you. From the minute I saw his face, I knew it. But you…I didn't think you'd let it happen."

"Nothing happened! Would you stop it?"

I didn't even know what I was denying or why. I was only defending my position, which was stupid. I knew damn well I felt something for Elliot. My mouth had betrayed me in that session; it hadn't lied.

"You're mine," he said, finger jabbing in my direction. "Nothing you do will change that. Nothing he does or feels will ever change that. He's temporary. He's a fucking leaf falling off the tree and dying. But we, you and I, we are the forest."

He was taking control of the situation and, apparently, the laws of physics as cars rushed to get out of his lane. More importantly, he was taking control of me by trapping me in a car.

"Slow down, or I'm bailing!"

He acted as though he didn't even hear me. "No. You're coming back. I'm shackling you to the wall until you understand that this is not a game. We're not teenagers. There is no puppy love, Fiona. Not for the broken."

"You know what? Fuck you!" The car was going about ninety when I opened the door.

He swerved, getting the inertia of the door to slap it closed. "Don't do that again!"

I popped my seat belt, reaching my foot over to his side. He tried to push me away, but I got it down on the brake. The car didn't know whether to stop or go.

Horns. Smoke. Swerving. Torque.

Deacon got his foot off the gas and pulled over, landing on the shoulder with a lurch. He turned on me.

He was mad. So mad he probably couldn't do more than shackle me. He'd never beat me when he was mad.

Maybe. Because I'd never seen him that angry before.

I wasn't ready to find out what he was going to do.

I snapped up my bag and crawled over the door, jumping to the asphalt.

"Fiona!"

I barely heard him as I ran into traffic. All the noises were loud. The screeching. The horns. The rap music coming from the white Honda that brushed against me. Even the movement of air around me was ear-squeezing. Deacon's voice existed in an indistinct middle ground. Only my breath was low enough to pay attention to.

Because fuck this.

I found the broken white lines between lanes. They were the only shapes that were solid in the indefinite blurs of cars.

These perceptions didn't even have a foothold in my mind. I didn't even think of them. I was in a now that was so short, I stopped wanting anything but to live. To get across, to get away.

Cars just stopped, once they could, and the air became thick with smoke and the smell of rubber.

"Fiona!" Deacon was getting closer, holding his hand up to a car on the fucking 405 and stopping it with his fucking will to make it stop for him, then loping toward me like he was just crossing La Brea with the light.

That was Deacon. And that power over people and physics was the biggest reason I'd given him control of my life. It turned me on.

It *had* turned me on.

A yellow Mazda lurched to a stop in front of me. A cab. The driver looked terrified, his brown eyes open to the size of doorknobs.

"Fiona!"

I'd somehow crossed three lanes of traffic, and Deacon was heading across lane number two.

I pointed at the guy driving the cab. "Can you take me to Holmby Hills?"

He didn't answer. I reached for the back door, and it was unlocked.

"Hundred dollar tip if you get me out of here."

He took off. I straightened myself as the knot of cars I'd tied up dissipated. Out the window, I saw a lady hold up a camera, taking a picture. And next to me sat a girl of about twenty, wearing makeup and a sparkly dress, two swaths of lipstick parted in surprise.

"Sorry," I said, "he can drop you off first. And I'll pay your fare."

She lifted a camera and snapped a picture.

chapter thirteen.

FIONA

Daisy asked me to autograph the back of a receipt she found in the bottom of her bag. I did it, leaving her a little note about how cool she was to share a cab with me.

"What's it like? To be you?" she asked as she folded up her precious paper.

"Pretty cool. I guess. I don't have anything to compare it to. You know, I got problems. Money's just not one of them."

"Yeah, you just got out of the"—she stopped herself and, whatever she was thinking, chose another word—"institution. Was it bad?"

"When they put you in isolation. That was bad. But otherwise, I guess it was all right."

I could have told her plenty about the drugs and the shitty woman psychiatrist whose name I forgot. I could have told her about being tied down or about the cameras everywhere. But I didn't know her, and all that seemed way too personal.

A voicemail came in from Karen. I listened to it while Daisy told me about her life.

*Me and Arrow are going to Baby's if you want to join. You should. We've been locked up too long.*

"I like being by myself," Daisy said. Behind her, box stores turned into cityscape as we zipped along the 405. "My mom is always on me to get another job. She has diabetes, so she can't work, and I have to drive her to dialysis clinic three times a week." I must have made a face or put on an expression that asked the question in my head, because she rolled her eyes. "Right, I'm in the back of a cab because I missed a payment and blah blah. I hate banks."

She made a little nervous laugh I hadn't heard until then, but once I noticed it, I realized she'd been tittering the whole time.

"So I take the bus, but if I make enough in tips, I pick up a cab home because the bus at night isn't really cool."

I almost told her I'd never actually ridden a bus, but I caught the words before they left my mouth.

"So you're headed home?" I asked.

"Yeah. Carthay Circle. I think wherever you're going is closer, so if you want to get dropped first…"

"It's Saturday." I said it as if every assumption should be obvious. The rest of the world partied harder on Saturday. Every day was more or less the same to me, but she must have adhered to the rules of normal people.

"Yeah?" she said.

"Aren't you going out?"

"No." She didn't look happy about it. She looked kind of down and lonely.

"I have an idea." I leaned over the front seat. The driver made eye contact with me in the rearview. "What's your name?"

"Basham."

"Basham, can you get off on Sunset? We're going to Holmby Hills."

chapter fourteen.

FIONA

Some things never changed. Parties always had the same ingredients: People. A pool. Music. Drinks. Drugs. Maybe some food. A few dozen people in white shirts picking up empties. Big Samoan guys frowning in the corners. Because you could get wild in the house, but you couldn't destroy the house. That cost money.

I lost track of Daisy sometime around my fourth Mojito High, which looked just like a mojito, but had pot leaves instead of mint leaves. I saw her by the pool with a drink, talking to Ivan.

My pager buzzed.

*—Where are you?—*

Deacon. Again. It was the seventh page like that. Just a question he felt entitled to ask.

Fuck his entitlement. Fuck his rules and his control.

"Fiona!" Jack called. "You have got to try this." He was still a nerd but a useful one, so the former Carlton Prep kids let him hang around their parties.

He crouched by a small mid-century table littered with sticks and flowers. A pile of what looked like mud sat in a saucer. Onna Michaels sat across from him, pinching her lower lip.

"My chin tingles," she said after Jack and I hugged.

"Give it a minute to travel down," he said, knee bumping like a jackhammer.

"What is it?" I said.

"*Catha edulis* hybrid with *ricinus communis* I was working on before I got stashed in the pokey. Concentrated it down in rubbing alcohol. Delivery method needs a little work. You tuck it between your cheek and gum. Calling it TarBaby." He pinched the mud, extracting a bit and bouncing his hand above the pile to loosen some black, fibrous strands. He held it up to me.

"Dude," I said, "I'm not your guinea pig. I gotta see what it does first."

"Gets you fucked up." He tucked the pinch into the front bottom fold of his mouth.

"Oh, man," Onna said. Her eyes rolled up, flicking and blinking to white. "Ah, that's good."

Gerald, another Carlton nerd who grew up muscular and fuckable, stuck his finger against his lower gum and said around it, "You found the key to the kingdom, Jack."

"Yeah," Onna groaned.

"When did you get out?" I asked.

"Week slash ten days," Jack answered. "Something like that. I'm thinking of going back in. There's a real market for this shit in the bunkhouse."

"Really?"

"Yeah. Chilton deals, but delivery is always a problem. He's paid off just about everyone who matters, but that front door's the toughest. He promised cash up front. He lets inmates pay him in trade. Girls and boys. He doesn't even care."

"He's sick."

Jack raised his eyebrow. "You some kinda homophobe?"

"You invent a new drug to sell to mental patients who pay in sex, and you're offended that I'm homophobic? Seriously? Warren's a sick fuck. Period."

But the argument was over. Jack's lips had gone slack and his eyes were half closed, revealing only white. He scratched his chin. Onna was welting her face and close to drawing blood.

Everyone in Westonwood would be walking around looking like they'd stuck their face in a shredder.

Yeah. The delivery system needed work.

I went out to the pool and nearly crashed into Karen.

I hadn't even seen her until then. Either she was too skinny or she had been busy in one of the bedrooms. But I squeezed her so tightly I could practically touch my opposite shoulders.

"How are you?" I asked, too excited for an answer. "You look great!"

She didn't. She looked like a fork. I was projecting my joy onto her.

"Staying at their place." She rolled her eyes. I knew she meant her parents. "Her and Dad can't decide where to take me. Dad thinks south of France and I'll eat because 'French food.' Mom says Aspen, because she wants to ski with her little drunk friends. They don't even ask me where I want to go."

"Where do you want to go?"

"I don't know."

"Figure it out, and we'll go together."

She smiled. "Yeah. I like that."

I kissed her cheek and we walked deeper out back.

Baby and Arrow were at a bank of couches with a bunch of other actors and industry douches. I found a spot and wedged myself in, joining the conversation about how long a guy's goatee should be.

I took a hit from the crystal bong going around. It was filled with straight Tennessee moonshine acquired from a busboy at Victoria's dad's restaurant. He supposedly had a still in his driveway. The shit tasted like tomato juice and rubbing alcohol, so we'd put it in the bong and smoked ecstasy-laced hash through it. The high was like a knife made of ice. It stabbed me in the spine and melted like cold water in my gut.

From the poolside couch, I entered another plane.

There was me.

And the Everything.

And the Everything pressed against me, hugging me.

I was safe in the Everything. Bound to it. When I shifted my body, it followed, molding to my movements, my dancing, my laughter, absorbing sound like a vacuum—a clear jelly mass nothing could penetrate. Not Arrow, who was kissing me with lips a million women died for. Not Derek, whose hands pressed my belly to him when we danced.

The Everything said it was okay to let them inside. I wasn't aroused. Not physically. I was just encased in joy and well-being and fucking was going to happen. Arrow, who had smoked from the same bong, carried me to a couch, legs wrapped around his hips. I was just starting to feel my feet. The Everything had released them first.

"Where's the bong?" I said.

Derek swirled the resin-brown moonshine. Arrow pulled a baggie from his pocket and tossed it to Derek. The music had started to cut through the gel of my awareness. I hated this song.

"What's in this?" Derek asked.

"It's vanilla. All I got." He looked down at me. His dick wasn't out yet, but it was on its way. "You in, Fee-Fie-Fo-Fum?"

"Let me get another hit."

"This stuff smells like asshole," Derek said, warming the bowl.

His voice grated on me, and the light from his Bic was too high and bright.

"See what Baby's got," Arrow said.

Baby Chilton turned around in her seat. Her turquoise hair was crimped, and her sunglasses were still on her head even though it was after midnight. She wasn't wearing a shirt, and her tits hung like silicone volleyballs in plastic bags. She'd had them done so many times, the guys said they could bite her nipples as hard as they wanted. She couldn't feel them anymore.

"I'm out," she said, turning to face us. "Holy shit! Fiona! When did you get here?"

She leaned over to hug me and landed on me before I could get up. She showered me with kisses, so I gave her a little tongue and a cheer went up. She got off me, and we sat.

Daisy stood nearby.

"You all right there, Daisy?" I asked, yanking my underwear from around my ankle. I thought I was supposed to be fucking someone, but I forgot to want it any more.

"Yeah!" she said enthusiastically. Good. Her drink was full, and she was smiling. That was all I needed to see.

"Give the new girl a hit," I said after I took mine.

Derek handed Daisy the bong. "Bowl's ash. Pack it or drink it."

"Shut the fuck up, Derek. You pack it." Fuck him. "She doesn't have shit. Your parents coproduce money-spitting Oscar bait every two years."

"I'm tapped, Fee-Fie." He put his hand on my knee. "You got some nuthouse shit you wanna share?"

"Can't smoke what I got."

"Oh my God!" Baby exclaimed. "I forgot to ask. Did you see my brother in there?"

Warren.

Her brother.

The hit I'd just taken went sour. My mouth tasted like the bottom of a foot. I wanted to go home.

"Yeah," I said.

"How was he?"

"Asshole as ever."

She snorted and lit a cigarette. A flake of ash fell on her left tit. She saw it and brushed it away. "They're talking about letting him out. Finally."

I had my phone out while she was talking about Warren getting out and the sick party that would commence. I didn't know what to do with myself. Sure, there would be a party and I'd be invited, but that wasn't the point. I didn't have to go. I could avoid him. It wasn't that hard.

Especially if I lived with Deacon.

My hands shook. I felt trapped in a matchbox. I held the phone to my face but didn't even know who to call for a rescue. My brain was stone soup. I knew there was an order to how to use the phone. This, then that, then the other, but I felt desperate and couldn't find the right little grey buttons.

Breathe breathe

Home button > green call button > code > contacts > Elliot Chapman

Now what?

I couldn't just casually ask if Warren was getting out without raising a flag. And hadn't I just told Elliot I loved him? Where was that fucking bong?

I stared at the phone. It was one in the morning. He'd be asleep. I didn't know where he lived. Lucky him.

I navigated to his number and hit SEND.

I wasn't even sorry in a way that necessitated an apology. I was saying I was sorry to myself.

Red button. Call ended.

"Drink it or pack it," Derek said from my right as Daisy still held the bong. He was so handsome, and his real-life persona was exactly the same as his reality-TV persona. Arrogant Hollywood douchebag. That was his brand.

I'd forgotten that I was about to fuck Arrow. I glanced at Arrow, who was chatting up Winny Sanchez. His hand was halfway up her skirt. We both forgot. That's how meaningful it all was.

Elliot called back. His name flashed on the screen with two options over the buttons.

Answer.

Ignore.

He'd answered. He'd gotten out of bed or rolled over and answered and missed the call and called back or whatever. He probably had crud in his eyes and hair all over the place. I wanted to stroke it back into place.

The song changed to one I liked, and I answered the phone.

"You called?" he said. "Is everything okay?"

"What are you wearing?" I purred or slurred. Maybe both.

He didn't say anything right away. I didn't like the silence. It was like having him watch what I was doing and shake his head with disapproval.

"We need to talk." His voice was clearer.

"We are talking."

"In person at a decent hour."

Fuck him for being right. And fuck him for being ethical, and for making me ashamed of wanting to know, ashamed of my high, of my hundred-dollar panties bunched on the floor, of the taste of Baby's mouth on me. What was I doing? Where was I? Why was I even here? And suddenly I was gripped with fear.

"Don't give me to another therapist."

"What?"

I glanced at my surroundings. Jesus. Where was I? Purgatory. Derek looked at Daisy expectantly. She swirled the hash-and-ecstasy-laced moonshine in the tube.

"Don't drink it, Daisy," I said. "You'll puke your guts up."

"But you'll be so fucking high you won't care," Karen said.

"Fiona? Where are you?" Was Elliot still on the phone? Had he heard me?

It was the third time he'd asked me that. Deacon, who was an early-to-bed-early-to-rise type when he wasn't hosting a party, was either awake, or hosting, or had these pages on a schedule, because his message came right after Elliot's question.

*—Where are you?—*

"I'm at a party in Holmby Hills," I said. "I can't find my underwear, and I'm so high. So. Fucking. High. Wanna come? I'll give you the address and you can—"

"Get a cab if you need one. Call me when you're sober."

He hung up.

*—Where are you?—*

*—Fucking sucking snorting. Thanks for asking—*

"Fuck you both," I said to the pager. I launched it into the pool. It dropped with a *plunk,* the cone of water collapsing into itself in slow motion.

Daisy still stood on the other side of the table, tilting the bong to her face.

"Give me that," I said, holding my hand out for it.

"Let her finish." Karen lit a cigarette.

Maybe it was because the famous-for-being-anorexic Karen Hinnley was defending her, but Daisy beamed a little and quickly, as if she wanted to do it without thinking about it, took a swig of the resin-saturated bong moonshine. Everyone groaned.

Bong water was bad. Bong moonshine was worse. Bong moonshine with the pure chemical happiness of Jump was more disgusting than I could imagine, and probably had never been tried before. Baby gave Daisy a bottle of water as she coughed. Everyone laughed. Even Daisy. Even me.

"You are about to get so fucked up," Derek said as he took the bong and gave it to me. "I salute you."

I put the bong on the table. "Who's got flake?"

Baby replied, "I got a couple lines' worth."

I held out my hand. Baby put a folded-up hundred dollar bill in my hand. I opened the bill, exposing the lovely white flake.

"What are you doing?" Baby asked.

"Can you get your dick out, sweetheart?" I said to Derek.

Collective laughter.

"Sure." Derek took out his cock. "You want it hard, you gotta work for it."

I rolled my eyes. "Stand up, stud."

I took it in my mouth. The taste of skin and sweat got rid of the sourness on my tongue, and I worked it until I thought he could maintain it. Some of my friends watched. Most had seen and done it all before, and it was boring.

"Man, you are good," he said as I stroked his cock with my hand.

Daisy stood watching, swaying a little.

"Too bad I'm not going to finish you."

"Ball-breaker."

"Stay still." I picked up the powder and tapped it onto his erection.

"Hey!" Baby cried.

I'd just dumped all her stash on Derek's dick, and I was going to snort it for spite. Because the last time I'd done that, I'd met Deacon. As I looked at the mess of powder on a douche-bag dick, I wondered…was I crying out for Deacon again? Was I trying to recreate the circumstances before he got my life under control?

My mouth already tasted like malice. Fuck this.

"All yours," I said to Baby.

"What do I get?" Derek cried.

"If you're nice, she'll let you come in her mouth."

Baby leaned down and snorted the coke off Derek's dick, licking off the last flake.

I wanted my pager back. My blood felt like gravel in my veins. I could call him. Them. Both of them.

Baby had left Derek hanging, and everyone thought that was pretty funny. I snapped up the panties and wiggled them back under my skirt.

Daisy laughed then puked. Karen got her Pradas out of the way just in time. I was going to have to get Daisy home. She'd have stories to tell, but I thought she might not. She seemed like a nice person. A person who leaves her boobs in her bra. Who didn't suck a dick in front of everyone for fun.

I looked at my phone. My messages to Deacon and my call to Elliot would give exactly the right impression and they'd be rightfully disgusted with me. They wouldn't know all the things I *didn't* do in Holmby Hills that night.

I'd felt this before.

This hateful unworthiness. My reaction to it was so ingrained I could predict it. The shame made me angry. The shame drew me into it and made me proud of what I'd done. I'd stand by it and deny it even existed. I stepped outside myself and saw myself the way others saw me, which wasn't new. But this time I didn't see the disdain and the worship. Nor did I internalize the thread of envy. I saw myself through Deacon and Elliot's eyes as if they were one man.

Surrounded by the music and the drugs, the stink of moonshine THC, the beautiful night, and the worthless humans around me, I sank into disgrace. I didn't run. I didn't cover it. Deacon would come for me. Elliot wouldn't.

"Fuck this," I whispered, pocketing the phone.

Next to me, Daisy was on her knees in front of reality star and winner of the genetic lottery, Derek Douchebag, and his cock was in her mouth. She was so fucking stoned she couldn't even keep her mouth open wide, and everyone found this funny.

"Derek, for Chrissakes," I said.

"What?"

"You got ten girls and a few guys you can stick it in. Leave her alone."

"Unless I can stick it in you, just shut the fuck up, Fee-fie Nuthouse."

I pushed him, hard.

He grabbed my wrist and bent it back. "Don't you fucking get judgy on me, you slut."

The bong stood like a twelve-inch clear phallus on the table, and there was nothing I could do but grab it and swing. It landed on Derek's head with a *thunk,* breaking in a wash of blood and brown-stained moonshine. He screamed and let go, dick suddenly flaccid. Everyone jumped back but Daisy, who didn't seem to know what had happened.

"You fucking crazy bitch!" Derek screamed. "You Drazen freak! You're all freaks! Crazy fucking freaks!"

God, Daisy had puke down her shirt.

I turned to Baby. "Sorry."

"Yeah. The Samoans'll take you out. Ping me next week if you want to hang."

I hoisted Daisy up from under her arms. She was no help at all, and I was halfway to hell myself. Derek was still screaming. Arrow gave him his shirt to soak up the blood.

Two gigantic men picked up Daisy and me, threw us over their shoulders, and put us in one of the party's hired cabs.

chapter fifteen.

FIONA

The penthouse suite of the Markham was dusty and unused. Total waste of a view and a pool. Mid-century Danish craftsmen had lovingly wrought chairs that hadn't felt the weight of an ass in months. It was all waste.

There were no paparazzi outside. I hadn't lived there in months. Likely they were outside Maundy. And certainly, they hadn't gotten wind of the night's drama, but they rarely did. Not the real shit. The real shit was like the mafia. No one talked.

That didn't change the facts.

It was my fault.

Nothing had happened that I couldn't have predicted.

From pissing off Deacon and Elliot, to acting like a fucking fool, to breaking Derek's face…even to Daisy, who wasn't prepared for a party without boundaries.

I'd wanted to hit bottom.

That was the plan.

Hit bottom and get seen doing it.

But Daisy threw me. And Derek Doucherson, who was just doing what Derek Doucherson did. I hadn't needed to open up his face.

"You don't hit bottom alone, do you?" I asked the elevator doors but made the statement to myself. *You don't do it alone.*

I owned the floor, so the elevator opened up onto a foyer and a door. Outside the door stood Debbie in a black suit. She stood so straight, she could have been a doll.

"Hey," I said.

"Hello, Fiona."

I punched my code into the door, and it clicked open. "Deacon send you?" I was way too sober for this conversation.

"Yes and no."

Her face told me nothing. She was implacable. She had to be. She'd grown up in a North Korean concentration camp where letting the wrong people know what you were thinking could get someone killed.

"You know who else has that thing you have?" I said as I opened the door.

"To which thing do you refer?"

She stepped in, and I closed the door behind her, letting the moonlight pattern the room in distorted rectangles.

"The thing where you make it so no one knows what you're thinking."

"Ah. Who else?"

"My sister. Theresa. It's like talking to a mask."

She stepped forward into the dark room until her face hit the light from outside. She looked different in that light. Sad, broken, held together with spit and chewing gum, every crack leading to the center of the earth. "Is this better?"

"No. Yes. But no."

"Do you know that you're loved?"

I turned on the lights. "Sure."

I knew it. I knew it like I knew how to hold my wrists when I was getting knotted. It was a fact, not a feeling. Not something that made me a better person. Actually, it made me feel worse for everyone else's wasted love.

"Want something to drink?" I asked.

"Water, please."

My kitchen had been used four times, so I had to look in all the cabinets for the glasses. I didn't have to search for the Advil for more than a second. I poured us water from the filtered tap I'd forgotten was there and gave her the glass from across the kitchen bar. She sat on a stool. I drank all the water and popped four Advil.

I didn't think ahead. I swam in the wake of any number of narcotics. My mind felt as if it was made of puzzle pieces that were in the right places but hadn't quite snapped together yet. I could make sense of my thoughts but not the space in between them.

Part of me wanted another line or another pull off a laced bowl. I'd always been impatient with the time between the high and the not-high. Can't sleep. Can't eat. Can't feel. Can't think. Might as well take another hit/snort/drink/whatever.

"Why didn't he come himself?" I asked.

"There's a crisis. In Eritrea, I believe. One of his photographers was drugged and is travelling with a group of ENA soldiers."

"Jesus. Those are problems." I put my glass in the sink. "Let me ask you something. How do you even deal with someone like me? You've been through so much, and you're so together. I've never had a real problem in my life."

She nodded, eyes on me. "If you shoot a man's chest and he's wearing a bullet-proof vest, he'll walk away unharmed. If you stab him, he'll be able to defend himself. But if you punch a naked chest, especially if that person is weak and vulnerable, the heart could stop. If you stab or shoot that chest, they are dead."

"Am I the naked chest?"

"All I can say is I have a vest on. What you feel pity about, my childhood, is what protects me. You were given nothing. You were free from want. From even the slightest anxiety. Now you have nothing to protect you. Every slap feels like a bullet wound. You tolerate more pain in your life right now than I do."

I couldn't help but look at her lips when she spoke, because I couldn't look her in the eye. She was validating my pain. She was giving me permission to hurt. Of all people, she was probably the one I needed it most from.

I got out two short glasses so I didn't have to face her.

Behind me, she continued. "In the camp, they took away my humanity from the day I got there. They made me an animal. So as an adult, every day, I have to choose to be human."

I opened another cabinet and grabbed the first bottle I saw, slapping it next to my glass. I pulled out the cork. I didn't even know what the liquid was except brown.

Debbie put her hand over her glass. "It was easy for me. The choice wasn't really a choice. It was life or death. For you, the privileged, you cannot believe you've ever done anything to deserve to be a part of this world. You're told you're royalty, but you don't feel it. You can't. Because you haven't chosen to be human."

She took her hand away, and I poured a finger of whatever-it-was into the glass.

"There was a girl with me tonight. Just a regular girl." I swirled the drink but didn't drink it. "I thought I'd show her a little fun. I'd take her out to a party and get her drunk on free booze and send her home in a cab. I thought I was doing her a favor."

I let my eyes linger on the amber liquid for a long time. Debbie didn't say a word, just gave me time and space to think.

"I think if I hadn't pulled her out of there, she would have died of an overdose with movie star jizz all over her." I tapped the edge of the glass on the marble counter.

"You took her to your Camp 22," Debbie said.

"I won't belittle what you went through."

"You're not. I made the comparison."

"I don't know what happened to me tonight. It wasn't fun."

"You don't have to go back to it."

"I can't stop alone. Not when I'm like..." Shit, I was crying. The thought of giving it all up by myself was painful. "Everything hurts, and nothing bothers me. I feel all backward. I get bored for five minutes, and I just want to go get fucked or fucked up." I rubbed my tears with the backs of my hand. "Then I run back to Deacon because he gets it all under control."

"You say you can't do it alone."

I sighed and looked at the whiskey. I didn't even like whiskey. "The last day, before I got out, I kind of felt good, because of all the work my therapist had done."

"The man I gave the shoes to?"

"Yeah."

"He's in love with you."

I sniffed a little laugh. "Yeah. He told me to get a cab. That was...wow."

"I bet it wasn't easy for him," she said.

I knocked back the whiskey and cringed. Breathed out hard. Corked the bottle. "I want to be worthy of Elliot because he has faith in me. And I want to be worthy of Deacon because of all the work he put into..." I stopped because I hadn't had the words until a few minutes ago. Everything clicked into place that night. "All the times he tried to get me to choose to be human."

"It gets easier."

"Yeah." I put the whiskey back in the cabinet. That little shot had done nothing for me. I had the tolerance of a hard-core drinker.

"I didn't come to save you," she said.

"No?"

"No." She drank the whiskey gently and quickly. Not a drop was left on her lipstick. "Deacon sent me to show you something specific, but I came to show you how to choose."

She stood and moved to the center of the room. I was on the other side of the counter without a clue as to what she wanted. She looked down and unbuttoned the loops of her tunic. She let the tunic fall down her arms, holding it by her fingertips for a split second before letting it drop to the floor.

Her hands stayed at her sides. Eyes downcast. I understood right away what she needed. We'd known Debbie the Domme, and she was utterly and completely a Dominant, but she'd only ever topped men.

I felt it. Everything Deacon had told me about. The arousing power. The anticipation of a slice of the world that was in my control. The throb of a need to bring a person to the edge for my pleasure.

"Debbie, I can't."

"I think you can."

Could I? I'd never considered it.

I'd had sex with women before, but the only time I'd Dominated one—not just topped, but Dominated—was at the Dome. Before Deacon, back when I did shit because no one was there to stop me, and even then, I wasn't in control.

I touched Debbie's nipple. Light brown on Asian-cast skin, it hardened immediately, and I rolled it under my thumb. I felt her breathe, watched her chest heave a little.

I untied her loose silk pants. They dropped below her navel. Under those silken dresses, she had a beautiful body, feminine and strong, with a long waist and narrow hips. With a flick of my fingers, her pants fell.

I thought to ask her if she was sure, but that would defeat the purpose of her request. I took her jaw in my hand and pulled her face up to look at me. She was so beautiful, and suddenly, the thought of having her was more than a lark. It was all I could think about. I kissed her, and it was lovely. The way she reacted to how I moved, submitted her lips to mine, let my tongue invade her mouth. She tasted like oranges. I'd kissed women before, but not like this. Not with purpose.

I took my mouth from hers and put her hands in mine. "Deacon told me he thought I wasn't submissive."

She surprised me by dropping her gaze, and I knew right then that I'd had no idea who she was. "He told you because I told him."

"I don't know what I'm doing."

"Yes, you do, and you don't need him."

I took a step back. Her words were so hard, so definite, and so correct.

Could I do this? Could I spend an hour dominating this woman? I didn't want to hurt her. She was precious to me.

Maybe that would be what made it work. At least for the next hour. As long as I didn't have to think past that, I could play this game.

"Take off my clothes," I said.

Looking downward, she unbuttoned my blouse. Her fingers on the placket were graceful and fine, and I didn't know if I'd ever been more aroused.

"We haven't set any boundaries," I said.

"I know."

I had to sound sure of myself. "Do you want a safe word?"

"My safe word is Pyongyang."

"All right." I hoped I'd remember it. At least for the next hour.

She slipped off my shirt, and I let her service me. Not helping, not hindering as she got on her knees and gently pulled down my skirt, then my panties. I stroked her hair when she ran her hands over my legs. I needed her comfort just then, but I was hesitating. That wasn't going to work.

"Stand up."

She did. We stood across from each other, naked but for shoes.

I reached for her breasts and ran the backs of my hands over them. So hard. Maybe as hard as my own. I pinched one nipple, twisting it. Her lips parted, but she stayed silent.

I walked around her, running my hands over her body. She was lovely. I just wanted to enjoy her without responsibility, but that wasn't why she was here. She'd come here to submit to me. I had a job.

"Back on your knees, beautiful," I said when I was in front of her again.

She dropped. I put my fingers in her hair, and she kissed my belly. *Fuck.* I could practically feel her lips on my clit even though she was nowhere near it.

Then I realized how close she was to seeing where I had been hurt. I didn't want her to see that. She'd know. Anyone who'd spent years as a Dominant would know. I scanned the room quickly. Her clothes were in a pile, including a red scarf. I stretched, grabbed it by the corner, and unwound it from the jacket

"Look at me." I had to suppress the need to say please. I didn't know where I'd gotten the compulsion to be courteous.

She looked up at me with her almond eyes, and I covered them with the scarf, knotting it behind her head.

I stepped back, halfway across the room, and sat on the floor. I bent my knees and spread my legs. "Crawl to me."

She did, putting her head down, letting her breasts swing. God, the things I wanted to do to those tits.

"Eat my pussy. Just your mouth. Lick it up."

She didn't hesitate but turned her head and kissed my swollen clit, then she drew her tongue along it.

"Suck on it."

She flicked her tongue over it then took it between her lips and sucked. I threw my head back. She licked again then sucked. My ass came off the floor. I was full, and ready, but more. I wanted more. More control.

I pushed her face away. "On your back."

She rolled over, and I crouched over her, knees on either side of her head. She looked at me in complete supplication, and I felt exactly right.

"Take my face," she said. "It's yours."

She opened her mouth, and I lowered myself onto it. "Take it. Eat it."

I rubbed myself on her face as she tried to grapple for control enough to make me come, sucking and licking whatever I let near her, pulling away then making her drown in me, until I shifted back and put my clit in her mouth.

"Suck it hard."

I landed on my hands as she pulled on my clit with her mouth, yanking a powerful orgasm out of me. I stiffened, clenched, rubbed myself on her face, and let go.

I crouched over her, panting.

*God, how did Deacon do this?*

*He got the fuck up and made sure I got what I needed.*

I stood, wobbly-legged, and moved the scarf off her eyes. "Bedroom's that way. Crawl in and get up on the bed. You're getting rewarded for that. Because it was awesome."

She smiled, face slick and shiny from my cunt. She twisted onto her hands and knees and crawled to the bedroom, head down, toes dragging in the high heels, ass swaying. I walked behind her, feeling a peace I barely understood. She knew how to do this. She was going to do exactly what I asked. Everything was under my control.

When she got up on the bed, she crouched on hands and knees, and I pulled her up to kneeling and kissed her.

"Are you all right with this so far?" I asked.

"Yes."

"I don't have any equipment or anything." I was expressing insecurity, and in the middle of the sentence, I realized what a complete buzzkill that would be for her. "So lean back and touch the headboard," I recovered. "Don't let it go."

I pushed her legs up and apart, letting my fingers drift down her belly into her wetness.

"I always loved your cunt," I said, putting two fingers into her. "It tasted like oranges." I put my fingers in my mouth and sucked on them. "Still does."

I reinserted them, then pulled them out with a swipe and a circle on her clit. Her eyes dropped, and her mouth opened.

"Here. Taste." I put my wet fingers in her mouth.

She sucked on them. I dug them into her throat. Three fingers. I wanted to enter her through my hand. To own her inside and out.

I knew what he felt, all those times, and I knew why it was nourishing for this little bit of the world to be mine.

I shifted over her and put my leg against her cunt until I felt its wetness. She curled herself around my leg, and we moved together. She sucked on my fingers and I pushed against her in ever-increasing rhythms. She looked at me, face scrunched, waiting.

I moved harder and faster against her. How much longer could I make her wait? She wouldn't come without me saying it was all right.

I wanted her to have the best orgasm of her life, so I made her wait as long as I could.

"Come," I said.

And she did, fingertips on the headboard, body arching forward then back. I'd never heard Debbie cry out in pleasure, and I'd seen her come plenty of times. But she cried out for me.

I felt like the queen of the universe, and for a moment, no more, I felt worthy.

I kissed her mouth when it was done and held her tightly.

"Deacon sent you to show me what it was like to dominate someone," I said.

"Yes."

"Should it feel like playacting?"

She sighed. "No."

"You knew I wasn't a Domme when you came here."

"Yes. But you know Deacon. You can't reason with him."

"So basically I'm just a horny perv?"

She laughed. "Yes. And you can do anything and go any-where you want. That comes from me, not the Master."

I rolled onto my back and looked at the ceiling. "Isn't it funny…technically I could always do whatever I wanted, but I think now I really can. And it's scary."

"Freedom can be frightening," she whispered, half asleep. "You're only free to choose how you're going to not be free."

Had I been scared that whole time? Had I held myself back from doing things because I was afraid? I tried to put myself in the shoes of my younger self. Back in Carlton Prep, when they'd tried to place me in college and they suggested business, I thought they were saying something for the sake of saying it, and I'd felt the walls closing in. Once I chose something, I'd be trapped in it.

Was I trapped with Deacon? Was his freedom a lie?

I could live without him. In the vulnerable place between wakefulness and sleep, between the submissive I thought I was and the Domme I'd just tried to be, I saw the truth. I didn't need him. But did I want him?

I was almost asleep when a voicemail came in.

Elliot.

*This is the deal. You show up at my office at eight sharp or I'll get you reassigned. There is no negotiation.*

Relief filled the place where the last of the tension had been, as if a drain had opened in the bottom of me and the ugliness fell out. I only had to wait three hours to apologize.

chapter sixteen.

ELLIOT

"This is the deal. You show up at my office at eight sharp or I'll get you reassigned. There is no negotiation." I hung up before I could soften it or backpedal.

That was risky. She was as likely to make sure she never saw me again as she was to make an effort to ensure I stayed in her life. But I didn't have any other cards to play. Threatening to put her back into Westonwood might give her exactly what she had been trying to get, if even subconsciously.

The clock said 7:58. Her call had come in seven hours ago.

I'd made the task of getting to the session on time almost impossible for my own sake as well as hers. I couldn't live with her troubles and addictions. She'd ruin me. Calling her in at eight o'clock was self-preservation at its finest. She'd miss the appointment, I'd recuse myself from her care, and that would be it. I'd find a life somewhere in the rubble.

The little light behind my desk flashed.

Someone was in the waiting room.

Did I have another appointment?

I opened the door. She stood there, sunglasses on, smelling of soap, fingers twitching.

"Fiona." I didn't have anything more to say. I was overwhelmed with relief that she hadn't let me push her away. I'd never wanted so badly for a plan to fail.

"Apologetic. Ashamed. Scared. Tired as hell," she said.

"Excuse me?"

"I'm using different words to describe myself."

## chapter seventeen

FIONA

I unloaded everything about the party, all its debasement and debauchery. I didn't sugarcoat it. I was honest. I'd never been so honest in my life. I didn't hold back a thing.

"My call," I said. "It was…I'm sorry. I wanted to hurt you, and yes, I got high and stupid, and I lost interest in the whole thing. I think it was because you weren't coming for me. It pissed me off, but it made me look at myself. And I was glad you weren't coming."

"So you went home?"

"Yes."

"What did Deacon do?"

"What did he do? Well, let's see. Apparently he was on his way to Eritrea, so he sent a mutual friend to fuck me?"

He raised an eyebrow.

"And I'm going to tell you what happened, but first I have to talk about the stupid thing I said to you yesterday and it was…did I say stupid?"

"What did you say?"

"I said I loved you. I think I meant it." Fuck this. I wasn't a high school kid with a crush. I was Fiona Fucking Drazen. "Actually, I know I meant it."

He leaned forward, just a foot or so closer, and I felt the space between us contract and pull at me, as if I could lean forward another inch and close the gap.

"Transference," he said. "It's when the therapist fills a gap in your life that you recognize because of the therapy."

I pressed my lips together and broke his gaze before it broke me. "Maybe. Sure. I was missing a therapist in my life and there you were."

I sniffed. Stupid snot was gathering in my sinuses, and I had to sniff to get rid of it. I cleared my throat. Looked at my hands, then at him. I felt like an ass.

"I shouldn't joke," I said.

He smiled. "Countertransference is when the patient fills a place for the therapist."

*Breathe. Breathe. You have to function. Breathe.*

"That sounds like normal people," I said. "You know, with needs. They meet each other and they fill needs."

"When you left Westonwood, I saw you by the door. I asked you to wait."

"Yes."

"You didn't."

"No."

"Why?" He asked it as if he already knew the answer.

"I told you right there. I'll destroy you. Men like you… you're nice. I'd eat you up and spit you out. I'd fuck you and leave you and—look, this isn't my ego talking. Nice guys don't last in my world. Nice guys with boundaries and common sense? I'm not paying for your therapy bills."

He laughed. I laughed.

Then he rubbed his eyes. "You knew how I felt. So you may feel vulnerable about what you said yesterday, but I opened that door. And the professional man in me regrets that."

"What about the unprofessional man?"

It took him a long time to answer. Two hours. Two minutes. Time folded in on itself. Could have been no time at all. But I saw every single thought cross his mind. A war raged behind his eyes.

"I promised myself before you got here that I wouldn't do this."

I leaned forward, putting up my hand. "Don't. You're right. Don't do this. I'm not worth it."

He looked me dead in the face, his hair a little askew, an expression so certain that he could have told me black was white and I would have believed him.

"But you are. You're worth all of it."

I sat back in my chair. "What do you want?"

"This session is supposed to be about you."

"That's the stupidest thing you've ever said."

"We're even then. In saying stupid things that are true."

"No. We're not."

Another two hours passed while he looked at me, and I fell into him. Maybe my feelings were transference, like he'd said, and maybe I was filling some gap in his life, but that didn't make it a lie.

Maybe it did, and I just didn't care.

As if we were pulled on the same string, he stood at the exact time I stood. He put his hand on my neck. I didn't realize I was cold until I felt the warmth of it. I leaned into his touch because it was so gentle, so firm, and I let him pull us closer.

"This is wrong," he said softly, as if giving it a name, accepting that name, and continuing.

I knew what he was doing, and I let him. Let his lips brush mine. Tasted the lemon water on his breath. Moved into the softness of his mouth, the wetness of his tongue as it entered me. His groan rumbled into my throat. I let him push our bodies together because I'd craved him from the minute I saw him. He understood me and he still wanted me, not in spite of my failings, but because of them.

I pushed my hips against him. He was hard. Very hard. Ready for it, and Fiona Drazen never turned down a hard cock. He pushed me against the wall, moving his mouth along my neck, his lips fire to the kindling of my skin.

I pushed him away, and we stood inches from each other, panting as if we'd run miles. I wasn't ready. I wanted more from him, but I couldn't expect anything yet. Not unless I wanted to ruin him.

"I can't," I said.

He smiled. "No. You can't." He kissed my cheek, lingering there, and I knew with a little prodding, I would have been on my back. Instead he whispered in my ear. "Not today." He ran his finger along my jaw and down my throat, leaving a path of tingling skin. "There's no looking back for me. So when I finally do what I've wanted to since I met you, that's it. No more fucking around."

I nodded and kissed him again. I didn't feel whole because of him. I felt whole because I'd chosen him.

## chapter eighteen

FIONA

When I was a girl, I had one place where I felt at home. Where I didn't feel eyes on me or pressure to be anything. I had to be perfect, but dressage had a set of rules for perfection I could follow easily and be done with when I got off the horse.

I got on the 110, down to Rancho Palos Verdes, where Snowcone lived. The smell of hay and horseshit was like home to me, and all the world slipped away.

"Hey!" I said when I saw Lindy arranging tack in front of the stables.

"Fiona!" She approached with a hug. "It's so good to see you. You look great." Lindy had Ivory Girl skin and straight brown hair she kept cut to the top of her shoulders. She hadn't aged past thirty-five.

"Thanks."

"I have the last of Snowcone's things all put together." She started walking inside, boots landing in a pile of mustard-colored horseshit. A true horse person, she didn't even notice.

"Excuse me?" I said.

"I love that horse, but she's yours, and you taking her is—"

"Taking her?"

"Did you guys get your signals crossed? Your boyfriend came and got her an hour ago. I went to see the Laurel Canyon space yesterday, and it's perfect."

"Yes," I said. "Yes, of course it is. Thank you, Lindy. Thank you for everything."

## chapter nineteen

FIONA

I had to remind myself why I was irritated with Deacon because I'd already forgiven him for taking Snowcone. I had nothing to offer my horse but neglect.

But that wasn't the point. What the fuck was Deacon doing in Los Angeles? He couldn't leave me alone for a minute. Who even knew what kind of clusterfuck he'd turned his back on in favor of watching me? Probably twenty journalists being held in a closet and his team was supposed to rescue them, but no. Fiona was on a bender. So he stayed to bring her horse to his stables.

Deacon was walking Snowcone around the pen. He was most comfortable in jeans and boots with a heavy button-down shirt. His forearms were wiry and taut, and his jeans hugged his hips as if they were made for him. Both he and Snowcone were well-muscled machines, and I sighed.

"Hey," I said, falling into step with them. "I thought you had something to do over there." I jerked my head in the way I did when I meant *Africa*.

"It can wait." He was full of shit.

"You couldn't have gone there and back."

"I didn't go. I got off the plane before it took off."

God. Fuck him.

"I'm mad at you."

"Why?"

"I never agreed to let Snowcone move here. This pisses me off."

"You don't sound mad," he said.

"I am."

"You're not. You're relieved. You have an excuse to stay."

He was so sure of himself. So measured. There wasn't a woman in the world who wouldn't fuck him, so why should I be any different?

"Does everything always make sense to you? Like, you want to keep me here, so you find a way to do it and that's that? I mean, I don't even know what I want, so you just think, 'oh, let me want something for her'? Is that what goes on in your mind? Is that your power trip?"

"Stop pretending you don't want to stay with me."

"I don't know what I want."

He stopped, yanking Snowcone back. "You want to be here, and you need to be here. When you leave, you party. When you party—"

"I stabbed you to get away from you!"

"You didn't stab me. The drugs did."

I pushed him. He didn't budge, but I pushed him again. I wanted to wake him up, to show him what he wasn't looking at. "You trapped me. You trap me with shit like this." I pointed at my horse.

"By being perfect for you?"

"By letting me run around like a whore."

"That's not what it was, and you know it."

"By being perfect for all of my worst impulses."

"They're a part of you. What do you think you're going to do now? Settle down in a ranch house in the Valley with a disgraced therapist? Have two kids and take Valium and fuck the pool boy behind his back?" His face jutted forward and his arm was thrown back, pointing at an imaginary house in a real suburb. "You're better than that."

"I'm not. I'm not even good enough for him." I swallowed, because I hadn't meant to say that. Not "for him," but my emotions had swarmed until there was no stopping the words.

"Really?" he said. "Did you fuck him yet?"

"It's not your business."

"You're right." In a flash, he had me by the back of my hair. He yanked it until I was looking into his piercing blue eyes. "It doesn't matter. It. Does. Not. You're mine. Your home is with me. And you can stab me another hundred times, and I'll bring you back. Because there is not another man on this earth who understands you the way I do and no woman who understands me."

"Let me go."

"Never." He twisted my body under him. His teeth were clamped shut, making his jaw stronger, tighter, more square. He was beautiful when in power and anger.

"I forgot…"

He dragged me to my knees. "Forgot what? This? How much you need this?"

"My safe word," I said. "I forgot it."

His reaction was immediate, and he let me go. I was still on my knees, hands in the dried leaves and needles.

"What's he going to do when you need to be broken?"

"Nothing." I got up, shaking from nerves. "He's not you. No one is."

"Do you love him?"

I didn't answer right away. I just stared at the face of the man I'd loved first, and would always love. I was hurting him. Every day I stayed with him, I cracked his armor, and if I left, I'd tear the armor away. It wasn't fair. He was too strong, too confident to let me do this to him. I didn't want to answer. I wasn't ready to own how it would affect him.

"Do. You. Love. Him?"

"No," I whispered.

He surprised me by smiling. "No, of course you don't. You can't."

He laid his hands on my crossed arms. Bone and sinew, with a squared joint at the base of the thumb. The hands of a man. Hands that bruised and tied, fingers that disappeared into my body. I couldn't deny them. My arms dropped to my side. I practically groaned when my throbbing pussy woke up. Elliot had left me unsatisfied, and here was Deacon, ready to take me.

"I don't want to be saved," I said. "Not anymore."

"You never needed to be saved. You only ever needed to be broken." He touched my lips with the pad of his second finger. "Remember this. Remember that you are not an average woman. You don't have average needs."

He leaned in until I could smell his rough scent, his dominance, and I went liquid.

"Open your mouth," he whispered.

I parted my lips. He put in two fingers, pushing to the back of my throat. I was mush. Oatmeal. The thought of his ministrations left me powerless.

"Anyone can fuck you," he said, fucking my mouth with his fingers. "I'm the only one who can break you."

I groaned against his fingers.

"Pull your pants down," he commanded.

I unbuttoned them and yanked them to mid-thigh. Cool air hit my ass, and I had a moment of worry that was chased away when Deacon spoke again.

"Pull your shirt up." He jammed his fingers down my throat, and I took them, choking as I pulled my shirt over my tits.

He grabbed a pierced nipple and pinched, pulled, twisted all at the same time, using the silver ring as leverage. The pain went right between my legs. He slid his wet fingers out of my mouth and put them between my legs, roughly running past my clit and hooking them into my cunt. I squealed. The pleasure was like a gunshot.

"You want me to fuck you, Kitten?"

"No," I gasped, every breath a lie.

"What does your wet little cunt want?"

"Break me."

He twisted my clit, and I screamed in pleasure and pain. I was close. So close, and when he rubbed my clit again, I came, standing in the middle of the yard.

"Get on your knees," he said.

I fell as if pushed by invisible hands, knees landing on the soft earth.

"Crawl to the stables."

Pants at mid-thigh, shirt hoisted under my arms, I crawled, eyes on the leaf-strewn ground, ass out in the air, a man behind me.

The last time I'd been like this—

I'd said no.

The last time I'd been on my hands and knees in a little forest, I was being ass-raped by a psychopath. But I didn't have to think about that. This would be different because I was with Deacon. I felt a pressure on my back. He pushed me with his foot. It was humiliating, but I was safe, and I was aroused with a heavy tingling below the waist.

In a way, I was also bored. I wanted to walk because it was more efficient, and I wanted to talk through my annoyance with him. I wanted to just fuck. Just get on with it.

The stinging pain on my ass was a surprise.

"Crawl, Kitten." He thwacked my ass with the belt again. "To the door."

I was lost in the act. My pussy was heavy with wetness and lust. Giving up all pretenses of control, I was exploding with desire.

As I crested the doorway to the stables, the leaves and dirt turned to wood planks.

"Stop," Deacon said.

I did. He walked around me, and I could see his muddy boots and the cuffs of his jeans. He swung the end of the belt in my sightline.

He crouched. "Look at me." His face was perfectly calm and in charge. His voice was even and sure. "I'm not threatened by any man. Not when it comes to you."

"Yes, Master."

He looped the belt around my neck tenderly, threading the end through the buckle. He reminded me of the safe sign we always used when I was gagged. "Snap your fingers to safe out."

And with one motion so swift and sure, he yanked it closed until I couldn't breathe. He pulled me up to kneeling, unbuttoning his jeans and releasing his beautiful cock.

He let me breathe. "Your face is mine to fuck. Open your mouth."

He tightened his grip on the buckle at the back of my neck and thrust his cock down my throat. It tasted of sweat and skin. I kept my mouth open while he thrust into it, using the belt as leverage, pulling my head where he wanted it. Keeping it still when he wanted to push his cock down my throat in repeated bursts. The world went black, and he loosened the belt, moved his dick, let me breathe, and started again.

I wasn't even there. God, I did need this. I needed to not have a will, not exist outside his pleasure.

He came down my throat, sticky and hot. I breathed through my nose and took all of it, because it was mine.

When he was done, he let the belt go, and I dropped down on all fours. My pants were still around my thighs.

"I thought I wasn't submissive." I said it coyly, trying to be gentle. It was a lousy time to try to prove a Dom wrong, but I couldn't help it.

"I smell the drugs on you. I only know one way to get the message across."

My scalp tightened as he took me by the hair and dragged me, dropping me on the carpet near a wooden X set into the wall. Each end had adjustable cuffs, and I went liquid as he dragged my wrist to an ankle cuff and pulled it closed. He stood over me, belt still looped in one hand, looking down at his property. I hated myself for disappointing him, and at the same time, I felt safe in his care.

"Don't cross your legs, and don't come," he said. "You sit there with your legs spread, and I'll let you come after I break you."

He walked out and closed the door.

## chapter twenty

DEACON

There was a reason I didn't fuck you for months when we met. I needed you to get control of yourself before I could control you. Otherwise there would be a lot of wasted effort. And you didn't seem submissive to me. The perfect body type for knotting, and from working dressage, you knew how to control your legs and arms, but you didn't seem truly submissive.

So I watched. I had control of you for that length of time.

The way you set your mind to it. The way you got on your knees for me. Fiona Drazen. We got all that coy sexiness stripped off you, and you were bare to me. Because of your public persona, you were more naked than anyone I'd seen before.

You blinded me like a bright light in the night.

I told you I was going to break you, and the night I did, I made the biggest mistake of my life.

chapter twenty-one.

*TWO YEARS EARLIER*
FIONA

"Breaking a submissive isn't an act. It isn't a result. Breaking is a process."

I looked at the floor. I was on my knees before him, hands behind me. I'd just seen my friend Earl at an afternoon birthday party that had seemed innocent enough. He offered me flake and cock. I had to run out like a schoolgirl to avoid snorting a line off his dick, but I couldn't stop thinking about it. Couldn't breathe from wanting it. Everywhere, the temptation to do things that would risk breaking what I was building with Deacon. I wanted it too badly. To be pushed off some kind of edge into controlled freefall.

"I still want it," I said.

"It's not something you want. It's something that happens when you're ready."

I didn't say anything. He put his fingers under my chin and forced me to look up at him.

"What's on your mind, Kitten?"

"Make me ready. Please."

From his face, I knew he would. I'd won. Whatever that meant.

## chapter twenty-two

FIONA

I'd gotten my back to the wall and my pants back up most of the way. Deacon had locked the cuff with a key and left me alone. He wasn't finished with me, but he had left me nonetheless. I was overcome with sadness. The bottom dropped out of me, a black feeling made worse from the dopamine rushing out of my brain.

He had to go. I couldn't deal with this all the time. This was the last fuck. He was out. Gone. Done.

I wanted him, and he gave me what no one else could, but he had to get out of my life.

Goddamn. After everything, I still wanted him to come back and fuck me.

My phone buzzed. I wiggled and got it out of my pocket with my free hand.

Elliot.

"What happened the day you left Westonwood?" His words were clipped, but the tones were a balm on my wounds. Any urgency surrounding Deacon went away in the smoothness of his voice.

"You stopped me at the door and chickened out."

"I had sessions after I saw you yesterday. Warren Chilton implied something in his group session that I need to confirm before—"

My blood curdled, and I cut him off before it went solid in my veins. "What kind of something?"

I heard a *tap tap* from his side. Pen on the desk? Finger on the counter?

"That he took something you didn't want to give."

I couldn't answer through my shock. He'd taken something I wasn't willing to give. What a nice way to say rape.

Elliot continued before I could answer. "And he smiles like a cat whenever he mentions you. And he mentions you too often."

I was tempted to deflect, just tell him Warren had gotten me sleeping pills and be done with it, but I didn't want to open that bag of shit until I could get a handle on the outcome.

"Maybe he wants to fuck me." I stretched out, wrist still bound to the bottom of the X. I was talking about Warren, but blocking him out with thoughts of my therapist made me purr.

"I don't doubt that, but there's something more to it."

He hadn't gotten the message, and that annoyed me.

"Isn't there some kind of rule about not talking about your patients?"

"I break rules with you. I'd break more. I'd break all of them."

"Doctor," I said, "you're not yourself."

"He's an antisocial psychopath who's fixated on someone I care about."

"Someone you want. It's different. You *want* me."

I heard him breathing. I'd downgraded our whole relationship after Deacon's exquisite humiliations, which was wrong. The light over Los Angeles was getting flat and grey in the late afternoon. Maybe Elliot and I were the only two souls awake in the world.

I waited for him to answer. Make up some lie about loving me or some bullshit.

"I want you," he said. "And I'm concerned."

"You want me?"

"You know that I do."

"What do you want?" I asked.

"You. The you you hide from everyone. You're under my skin. I can't live with myself until I make your world right and share it with you."

I lowered my voice so he'd get it. "That's not what I meant. What do you want *to do* to me?"

Another pause. This one shorter.

"You want to do this?" he challenged me.

"Yes."

"I want to fuck you." He roared a little. Like a lion prince who could grow to be the king of the jungle.

"How?" I clicked the speakerphone on and put the phone down. "Tell me. I'm all alone here."

"How?" His voice had changed, as if he'd made a decision to engage in this game. "By bending you backward on the kitchen table. By holding you down by the throat and pulling off your underwear. Spreading your legs so far apart. Then eating your pussy. It tastes like honey."

I throbbed. His tongue on me, sweet flicking softness on my cunt. I put my fingers under the crotch of my underwear. I was soaked. Slick.

"God, yes. I want that."

A laugh of relief escaped his throat. He'd taken a risk by engaging in this conversation, I knew that.

"I don't let you come. But you get close. I can feel you tighten on my tongue."

"Fuck me," I said.

"Are you touching yourself?"

"Yes. Don't stop."

"I pull your knees toward the table. I can see your cunt. It's beautiful. I slide my dick along it. You're so wet for it."

I heard him swallow. "Fuck me, Elliot. Just fuck me."

"You're so tight. And you look at me. You feel so good."

"I'm going to come."

"Yes."

I tightened around my fingers, pulling against the cuff that held my wrist. It was a good one. A warm wave over my body. Just as I heard him groan, the phone fell, skidding away when my foot lost leverage and kicked from under me.

I stayed sprawled there, breathing hard, looking at the ceiling as it turned dark grey.

"Fiona?" Elliot called from the phone.

I twisted to get it but couldn't reach. "Yeah."

"Where are you?"

"I'm at Deacon's. I can't reach the phone."

"What do you mean you can't reach the phone?" he asked.

"He cuffed me to the wall."

"What?"

"Take it easy. This is not a big deal," I said.

"What do you mean it's not a big deal?"

"It's the kink, Doctor E. Like phone sex. Stop being a prude."

"I'm coming for you." Somewhere in his world, a door slammed. Keys jingled.

"You don't even know where I am," I protested.

"You underestimate me, and you underestimate what I'm willing to do for you."

"I don't even know what that means."

"He couldn't just take you past the gate without saying where he was taking you. You're still an outpatient."

"Please don't come here," I said. "It's not going to be okay."

"It is going to be okay. It's going to be better than okay. I'm giving you permission to make it okay. And me, I can't live like this anymore. I can't settle anymore. I spent my entire life holding back. That's why I almost entered the priesthood. And I love God. I do. My faith is real, but my vocation wasn't. I used it so I'd have rules to follow to keep me in line."

"You see what happens when there are no rules, Elliot. You end up like me. I'm not what you want to be."

"I don't want Yesterday Fiona. I want Today Fiona. Tomorrow Fiona. We can break the right rules together. I got through that session yesterday with you, and I beat off like an adolescent. And when I went over to Westonwood and heard what they were saying—I want to kill him."

"You're crazy."

"I am."

I didn't answer but closed my eyes. I was used to being wanted by friends and strangers. Deacon protected me from those who wanted me by letting my world revolve around his, deflecting their desires and putting them under our control.

But Elliot was different. We'd met without Deacon's protection. He'd spoken to me in a way no one else had. I believed him. He may have been misguided or wrong, but he meant what he said.

"I don't know how I feel," I finally said. I'd committed myself to putting Warren down, and that goal precluded me from getting closer to Elliot, phone sex notwithstanding.

"I'll be there in fifteen minutes."

Deacon's voice cut through the room. "You're going to get an eyeful, doctor."

He entered in trousers and a button-up shirt, carrying a wooden paddle over his shoulder.

Without missing a beat, Elliot answered, "Let her go."

"See you later." Deacon scooped up the phone and hung up, then he slipped it in his pocket. "Well, Kitten. How was your afternoon?"

Deacon was in fine form, dropping the paddle to his side and tapping his knee. It had three large holes in it to cut air resistance.

"Fine, Master."

He tucked the paddle under his arm and unlocked me. I could smell his soap. He'd showered for me.

"You touched yourself," he said as he turned the key. He didn't say how he knew—he just did.

"I'm sorry. I wasn't supposed to."

"You never have. I'll restrain both hands next time."

I was on the floor, and he stood above me. I was afraid, and it was the fear and the anticipation of pain that turned me on.

I was wet all over again. Yet it seemed too soon for the paddle. The paddle was the end of the line for me, and he was starting with it.

"Put your back to me. Hands over your head."

I did it, holding two thoughts in my head at the same time: that I was worthy of Elliot and that I was a piece of meat for Deacon to use.

"Master?" It felt weird, slipping back into that role. Part of me wanted to curse him and tell him to fuck off, which was how I knew he was right. In his eyes, I needed to be broken again.

"Yes?" He pulled my pants down just below my ass.

I was going to ask him his intentions, but that would have been out of line. I'd forgotten that in the space of an afternoon. "Where do you want me?"

He pointed the paddle at a white painted picnic bench. "Knees straight. Hands on the seat."

I did as he said, putting my ass in the air, and I wondered, despite all agreements to the contrary, could I just get up and walk away? As long as my mouth was free and I could utter my safe word, would he still do this?

"What did the doctor want?" he asked.

He pressed the wood to my ass. *Tap tap tap*, warming me up.

"To fuck me."

"Did you let him?"

"Over the phone."

The paddle landed on the backs of my thighs, and I bit back a scream.

"I could tell you'd climaxed as soon as I walked in. Thank you for being honest. But you didn't ask me first."

He hit me again. So soon after the previous smack, with no break between, no chance to breathe, my skin was on fire. I locked my jaw closed and grunted.

"You're out of control," he said, paddling me a third time.

My knees bent under me, and tears flowed. "Yes, sir," I grunted.

"We're getting it back. You and me. Count to twenty."

"It's too many!"

"Twenty-five then. And keep it quiet. Willem's here."

The paddle landed with an explosion of pain. My knees buckled, and I counted.

chapter twenty-three.

*TWO YEARS EARLIER*
FIONA

Once I'd decided to let him break me, it didn't get any easier. I didn't understand the concept. Didn't internalize it because I wanted it.

Number Two Maundy was packed to capacity. It was the heyday before the accident that killed Amanda. Before Deacon left that time, when he was still as committed to getting me under control as I was.

I was naked, face down, swinging three feet above the floor, legs spread below me, hands twisted behind me. My ass was up, and my ponytail was knotted behind my head, forcing my face up. I saw myself in the mirror, little tits making wide Vs under me. Some of the guests watched, some didn't. Some were in their own humiliations. But I was in the center of the room, drooling around a ball gag, taking the paddle, and crying. The bottom of my face shone with snot and spit, and Deacon had rolled up his shirtsleeves.

"One last, Kitten."

I barely heard him. The last *thwack* was all I heard as my vision broke into fragments from the pain. When I came back, I saw him. Mister Rugged, from my first trip to Maundy, was rolling whiskey around the bottom of his glass.

Deacon came in front of me and faced me. I was at crotch level, and he bent to look me in the eye.

"Not broken," he said. "What do I have to do?"

The question was rhetorical. He'd told me exactly what he was going to do, and I'd agreed to it. He said I was safe, that he'd be close by. I wasn't even scared.

He popped off the ball gag.

"Break me," I begged. "Please."

"I can't, it seems. It takes a village."

He clapped twice. They were taking me. They were all taking me. I looked over at Deacon, who had stepped back and crossed his arms. He was there, watching.

Mister Rugged stepped up first. He shook hands with Deacon, and they spoke a few words in a language I didn't know. Then he looked at me.

Behind me, someone cupped my burning and wounded ass.

"Defiant one, you are," Rugged said.

He slapped me, open-handed. I was stunned, even past the scalding pain behind me. I twisted in my restraints, but I was fastened tight by Deacon's knots, and the more I moved, the more my hair felt as if it would get ripped from my head.

"Oh, this?" He slapped me again. "This bothers you?"

It did. He put his fingers down my throat and slapped my cheek with his other hand. No, I did not like this. The cock sliding into my lubed asshole? I could take that any time, but when Rugged slapped my left cheek, a piece of my heart broke off.

"He's too nice to you," he said, jerking his head toward Deacon, who must have moved behind me. "You're just a little fucktoy, and he treats you like a woman."

He removed his hand from my mouth. I choked and gurgled out a glob of spit. He slapped each cheek. Palm. Backhand. Like it was nothing.

I wanted to say my safe word. I didn't think I could stand him doing it again. I was humiliated, but not as a sex object. I could take sexual disgrace and eat it for lunch. But now I was degraded as a person. A human. His slaps weren't sexual or personal. They were detached, public, shameful. My nudity and my position were stripped of their power to seduce. And that was where I lost myself. I broke like a handful of spaghetti, right in the middle, pieces flying away.

He put his dick in my mouth and I took it down my throat, while someone I couldn't see fucked my ass as if I wasn't even there.

And in a sense, I wasn't.

I'd gotten myself in too deep on Maundy. I'd asked to be broken. Begged. Maybe it was the novelty of the idea, or maybe it was a real kink. But I dropped out of those ropes changed.

I was bone-tired. Cold. Aching everywhere. Sticky with the juice of half a dozen men. When Deacon tried to touch me, I thought I'd be physically ill.

"Get away from me."

Someone scooped me up and took me to the Care Room. I didn't want to be there. It was too generic a space. Like a hotel room for anyone stuck in subspace. I hated it suddenly, and wanted to be in a personal space that wasn't accessible to any sub who needed aftercare.

But I was too wrecked to protest. I was laid on the clean white sheets in the windowless room. I shivered. I didn't know I could be so cold. Candles were lit.

Soothing music came on, and a lovely female voice said, "Welcome to the world of the broken." Debbie covered me with a down blanket. "You were always lovely. But right now, you are most beautiful."

She sat by me and stroked my hair. I felt isolated, alone, floating in the stars, miles above the movements of the human race.

## chapter twenty-four

FIONA

I wasn't broken during the paddling in Laurel Canyon. My ass hurt, and I was annoyed. I was waiting for Elliot to show up and make a scene. Then I would have to act quickly to defuse it.

"Twenty-five!" I said through gritted teeth, more relieved that we'd get to do something else than that I'd reached the end to the pain.

He tossed the paddle aside and pushed me down, pushing my face into the bench.

"Remember how I broke you last time?"

I couldn't answer from the pressure on my jaw.

"Desexualizing you." He put his other hand on the open wounds on my ass, digging in his fingers. "Same thing rarely works twice."

He pulled back, getting both hands on my bottom, and pulled the cheeks apart. I didn't know what he intended, and I never found out. Because he got a look at what was going on back there, and the cruelty dropped off him.

"What the—?"

"Wait, I—"

"Who did this to you? The fucking doctor?"

"No!"

He yanked up my underpants. Angry. Tender. All the things at once.

"This"—he indicated my body as one violated unit—"I've seen everything. This was not consensual. Fiona. Kitten. What happened? What did he do to you, and why are you protecting him?"

Deacon was always in control, but standing over me as I adjusted my pants, he exhibited a level of confusion and pain I'd never seen before. It was like the earth shifting beneath me. If he didn't know what to do, then every action I'd considered taking must be wrong.

Right before my eyes, all the confusion congealed into rage, and I feared for my friend, my plan, and my Master.

"Leave him alone." I could have denied further. I could have told him it was Warren, but I did a calculation faster than I ever had, and I made a choice to build a wall around Elliot. "I will rain hell on you, Deacon. I love you, and I will ruin you."

"Are you threatening me?"

Again, the confusion. Recognizing it for the second time, I knew what his confusion turned into when it transmuted into a solid emotion.

I said nothing. I held my hands at my sides, paddled ass waiting for the aftercare that wasn't coming. Wanting to let him hold me and care for me, to kneel before him because it would make everything all right. I wouldn't have to take responsibility for a damn thing. It would just work itself out in the form of violence.

A knock at the door, and a voice through it. Willem. "There's a guy at the gate."

He barely had the sentence out before I ran past Deacon, opened the door, and blew past Willem, past Debbie gathering fallen oranges in the yard, through the front house, to the driveway, which I took in loping strides, barefoot on sharp stones, and opened the pedestrian gate.

Elliot waited in his car.

I yanked on the door handle. "Unlock it!"

*Clack.*

I threw myself into the passenger side. "Get me out of here."

"What—?"

"Go!"

He backed out of the drive, little car spitting pebbles, and got on Mulholland. I turned my body around to see if anyone was following.

"Are you okay?" he asked.

"I'm fine." The coast looked clear for the moment.

"What happened?"

"Deacon thinks you raped me."

"*What?*" He skidded onto the shoulder.

"Keep driving!"

He pulled back onto the road. I twisted again, looking for the private road to spit out a black Range Rover.

"You told him I raped you?"

"Of course not. He saw…" I sank in my seat.

"What's happening?

"Just drive. Please."

"Where are we going?"

"You tell me."

"Fine," he said, as if making the decision was more of a relief than a burden.

He took a left, then a right, then a series of turns I'd never remember, heading deep into the basin. We didn't talk. There was too much for me to know where to start, where to end, what to tell him, and what to hide.

## chapter twenty-five

FIONA

Elliot pulled up to a meter on Wilshire, set the wheel to its straight position, and put the car in park. He tapped the gearshift and said, "You're squirming in your seat."

"I got twenty-five with a paddle."

He looked at me.

"That turns you on," I said. It wasn't a question.

"My dick is the last thing on my mind."

"But it reacted."

He stepped out of the car without confirming, and walked around to my side. He opened my door. After I got out and he closed it, he guided me into a little coffee house.

He whispered as I passed, "Everything about you makes my body react."

I smiled at him. "I'll have a buttercup. No sugar."

I sat at one of the lacquered teak presswood tables under the hardware store buckets hanging from the ceiling. A bonsai tree sat in the center of each table and along the bar, and the Korean love ballads were loud enough to shield our words.

He put my cup in front of me and sat. I stirred the fat into marbling spirals in the black sludge.

"Thank you," I said.

"Do you want to tell me about Warren?"

I nodded, biting my upper lip. My eyes filled up. I hadn't told a soul, and admitting it made it real. I didn't look at him. I said the words to the swirling pat of butter in my espresso.

"By the creek. He hurt me badly enough for Deacon to see two days later. I said 'no.' I said, 'lube me up,' something, you know? Just…it was bad enough sitting still for it. Having to because no one would believe he raped me. But it hurt. Having him call me a whore who liked it. Because I had. I'd liked it like that often enough.

"It was so bad. It hurt inside. In my guts. I felt like I was getting ripped up. And he just…he felt like having anal and I was there. It wasn't that he liked that it hurt me. He just didn't care. I was invisible. I died. I feel like I died."

Elliot put his hands over my arms and tightened them around me. He didn't say a word.

The weight of it was too much. The flat grey mass of sadness broke me again. I should have broken that day behind the fence. I should have gone into subspace and had aftercare and walked out a shiny strong new woman. But I'd been holding myself together, and in that coffee shop in Koreatown, I was falling apart, leaking all the garbage and reeking toxins that I'd carried. My humiliation and pain spilled onto the cracked sidewalk with the rest of the trash no one picked up.

But it wasn't done. Maybe the valve on the bucket had been loosened. Maybe the pressure was relieved enough to continue with my head on straight.

I pulled away a little.

"You have to know it wasn't your fault," he said.

I nodded, but I didn't believe him. A part of me would always wonder how much my history had played into Warren's decision, and how much I should have expected from a guy who sold amphetamines to an anorexic. I always said I was smarter than that. Better equipped than the girls who woke up on the beach with their panties missing and blood under their fingernails. Sharper than the ones who had to abort fetuses with mystery fathers.

Maybe not.

"What do you want to do?" he asked.

His fingertips brushing my palm was sexual but comforting. He wanted me. You didn't need to be a rocket scientist to figure that out. But he wouldn't try to fuck me. Not while I was talking about rape. Not as long as the pall of inappropriateness hung over us.

"Nothing," I said.

"Nothing? You're going to let him get away with it?"

"I never said that."

"You need to tell someone."

"Who? His father owns the mayor's office. His mother? In Carlton, he cornered Robbie Sanchez in the bathroom and fistfucked him in front of the entire lacrosse team. Literally fistfucked him. Warren's mother decided he was pushed to do it, and guess what happened?"

"Robbie got suspended."

I put my finger on the tip of my nose.

"You're not a Sanchez," he said, running his thumb along my arm. "You're a Drazen."

"I'd rather take care of this myself."

"How?"

"I'm still deciding. But I'm pretty sure I'll run over anyone who gets in my way."

He nodded, as if accepting not only that I wasn't making an empty threat but that the threat could be directed at him. "I won't get in your way."

"You might."

He tilted his face toward me. "No. I don't think I would. I know what it meant for you to tell him no."

There was something strong and sure about him. Something overtly understated. I could love him, maybe. But not for long. I'd ruin him just for the challenge, even if it broke my heart.

He took my hand and squeezed it. His hand was dry and strong without hurting mine. The touch was tender without seduction.

"Again, it wasn't your fault," he said.

"How do you even know that?"

"Because there's no shame in you. If you wanted to do it, you'd just say so and tell everyone to fuck off."

I spit out a laugh that turned into a quick inhale and a sob. I pulled my hand away and covered my face. I didn't want him, or anyone, to see me cry. I wanted to be the one in control for a fucking change.

"I want to die," I said between my hands. "Like, really die."

"I won't let that happen."

I took my hands away from my face. "Elliot, come on."

"What?"

"You're not the type to be able to stop anything from happening to me or anyone else."

"The type?" He tapped the end of his spoon on the napkin, carving a stack of fading taupe frowns.

"Sweet guy. Sensitive. Measured."

He smiled at me. "Of course. I get it. A nice, measured guy can't protect you."

"A God-fearing, rule-following guy. And maybe that's the point. If I wanted someone to protect me, Deacon would do it."

"But you didn't tell him."

"I can't protect him. See, he gets a lot of things about the world and how it works. He's seen a lot of scary shit and... you know...done scary shit too. But he doesn't understand my world. Not even a little."

"You shouldn't handle this on your own."

"There's nothing to handle," I lied. I'd led him too close to my center and wanted to throw him. "I just have to deal and move on."

"A minute ago you wanted to die."

"I'm not known for being consistent."

He leaned against the wall, put his ankle on his knee, and tapped the table. "When we met, I wanted to make you better. I want to make everyone better, but you? I wanted to reach inside you and heal whatever it was. Now I think it's all flipped around. I want to wipe the evil off the face of the earth so it's safe for you. But I'm not the guy who's going to decapitate Warren Chilton. Because I know how his world works." He jabbed the table as if his point was there, and he turned his upper body to face me. "I know his status, and I know he's going to do it again. So he's not getting away with it. I promise you, because you have this face on like it's fine, but a minute ago, all your hurt spilled out. This fuck isn't getting away with shit. His life's going to be a living hell inside that place. Isolation's going to be a cakewalk."

"I don't want you to get involved."

His phone rang, and he pulled it out. He looked at the screen, smiled, and showed me the readout.

*FIONA*

"Too late, princess."

Shit, Deacon had my phone. I grabbed for Elliot's, but he pulled it away.

"Hello?" he said as if he didn't know who it was. "Yes, this is Doctor Chapman. We've met."

"Jesus, Elliot, come on."

I grabbed for the phone, but he turned away. Was he enjoying this?

"She's here. She looks beautiful, by the way."

"Do not bait him!"

He glanced at me then put his hand over the phone. "Why not? Are you afraid of him?"

"For your sake, I am."

He shook his head and put the phone back to his ear. "She's fine. You don't have to worry." Pause. "What's that supposed to mean?" He leaned back in his chair again.

Fucking men. You'd think they'd both pissed on me like a hydrant.

"I would never take what wasn't freely given. I think you know that." Elliot just smiled as if Deacon had said something particularly amusing. "I'll take that into consideration." He handed me the phone. "He wants to talk to you."

I took the phone. "Deacon."

"Come back. Come back now." He used his cold, Dominant voice, and it went right to my very soul.

"I can't."

"Kitten, you are in no place to get your life under control, and that man you're with is not qualified to keep you safe."

"Safe from what?"

"Yourself."

*Fuckhim- Fuckhim - Fuckhim - Fuckhim*

I hit the red button to cut him off and plopped the phone in front of Elliot.

"You all right?" he asked.

"I left my car at Laurel Canyon."

"I can get it for you."

"No. I want to go to my condo in Malibu. Can you take me?"

"Sure."

## chapter twenty-six.

FIONA

He took the 101 and dropped down through the mountains, over Las Virgenes because PCH was always a disaster. He didn't even tell me he was going around the civilian route. He just knew the best way to get to my place the way he knew how to get to me.

Estates hid behind hedges, and Bentleys stopped at lights, next to circa 1977 Chevys. Elliot had one hand on the wheel, fingers articulated and active when he turned it.

I didn't know what I wanted from the man. Maybe I wanted to destroy him. If that was the case, I'd certainly set on the right path.

"I don't want to freak you out," he said, "but I want to tell you something. Or some *things* before I even get you to your place."

"I'm a captive audience. But Doctor Chapman?"

"Elliot. Please."

"Whatever you say, it won't change anything."

Undaunted, he continued. "The first thing is, I'm as confused as you imagine I am. I shouldn't be doing this. You're considered my patient for at least two years after our last session. I shouldn't even let you in my car, much less track you down in Laurel Canyon. Much less call you. I'm risking everything. My license. My reputation. My jobs. And I know I'm going to walk away with nothing. I'm fully aware that either you're going to hurt me or I'm going to have to start my life over from scratch as a short-order cook or something. There really is no other way around it. I accept that. I'm a martyr for you right now."

A big package wrapped up in a bow. Ten tons. No sound from inside. My name written in fancy script on the tag. That was his life, and he'd just handed it to me. It wasn't even my birthday or Christmas or anything.

I didn't know if I wanted it or not. It was just a heavy box. But I couldn't give it back, couldn't thank him for it, and I wasn't ready to open it. Not yet. Its presence in my life was too overwhelming.

"Have you thought about why?" I asked. "Because there's no reason you should feel this way. I couldn't be more wrong for you."

He stopped at a light and looked at me. "Do you play chess?"

"I used to play with my sister. She creamed me."

The light changed, and he pulled forward. "The biggest learning curve in chess is the opening. Your first few moves. Your initial choices decide the game. With every move, nearly infinite options turn into fewer and fewer options until you're cornered. Or your opponent is cornered. You go from infinite possibilities to despair in fifty moves as a result of the first five.

"Life isn't like a game. Of course you go from board to board your whole life. You start over, make moves, options get limited, et cetera. I don't want to make big analogies that don't work. But I want to say, I was at my endgame until you walked into my office."

He stopped. I looked out my window.

"Am I talking too much?" he asked.

Was he? I'd gotten lost in the sound of his voice. I heard the words, I listened, but something in the way he put his syllables together clicked for me. I could listen to him all day.

"We're not on the clock," I said. "It's your turn to talk."

He paused as if considering the next part of his speech. "I was cornered. I had nowhere to go. And when you came in, I didn't understand it, but you felt like a way out. An open window. When you came in, the traffic cleared and I had an open road in front of me. Why? I don't know. Maybe because you were an escape hatch, or maybe because we're doomed. But you feel like a puzzle piece, and when you talk or move, there's something about it that clicks in place with me. I can only feel it, and no piece of paper or degree or job or anything is going to turn me back.

"The game changed when I met you. God help me, I am not going back to checkmate. I'm playing this board. I'm making my opening moves. I have never felt so awake, so alive, and yes, I'm going to call it like I see it. I'm not making you any promises. I'm not pretending this makes sense. But I feel closer to God when I'm with you, and that has meaning to me."

Inside the hum of his voice, breathing the comfort of it, I felt the weight of my responsibility to him.

I waited until he had to stop at a light before I answered. "I'm very hard to love, Elliot. I don't want to hurt you."

He took my hand and squeezed it. "I'll let you do it, but I'm not going to make it easy."

"I'm not sure where I am with Deacon."

He looked me in the eye and squeezed my hand harder. "He's in your past. You get a new board too."

Did I? Would I ever get a fresh start? I hadn't considered that I would ever deserve one, but there I was, with the light green and the freeway open wide before me.

## chapter twenty-seven

FIONA

It was night when Elliot pulled up to the Markham.

"Thank you," I said.

"What are we going to do about Warren?" Elliot asked. "He's getting out next week."

"Once he does, I lose control of the situation, don't I?"

He tapped the steering wheel. "No. I do."

"I'm not dragging you into this." I turned in the passenger seat so I could see him. "The reason I didn't tell Deacon was because he'd hurt himself trying to kill Warren. I don't want that for you."

"And I don't want you going after him."

His eyes lost their color in the shadows, but his jaw became more defined. Straighter, stronger. I touched the line of it, down his neck, flattening his collar. He took me by the back of the neck and pulled me toward him. Our lips crashed together, tongues twisting, groaning, bodies finding each other. He put his hand between my legs and pressed my pussy through my jeans. I was damp through the fabric. He curled his fingers along the seam, and I threw my head back and moaned.

"Fiona," he said, his voice husky, "I want to see you come."
He pinched the front of my jeans under the fly, pressing my clit.

I wanted him to make me come. I wanted him inside me. He pulled me to him until his lips were at my ear.

"Leave him," he whispered.

I knew that if I said I would, he'd take me right in the car, and I'd bring him upstairs and we'd fuck all night.

And would I leave Deacon?

Maybe. Maybe not.

"Not yet," I said, backing away.

"When?"

I kissed him on hard on the lips and got out of the car.

chapter twenty-eight.

FIONA

*You told me you could see the connections between people. Just like an observational thing. The time you did my aftercare. Remember, Debbie?*

*Yes. I remember it.*

*Have you seen a connection with Deacon and me?*

***

I went into my bedroom and strode right to the closet. It had double racks of clothes and two rooms with windows. I'd had it lined in camphor, and the sharp scent woke my sinuses. I opened a floor cabinet and spun the dial of the safe. *Whush.* It opened, and there sat some jewelry, a black card, and a few envelopes of cash. I also had pills, mostly tranks, and a few vials of flake for emergencies. Was I going somewhere?

I needed money and my car. Right. The black card was right in front of me, and the keys to the car were with the valet downstairs. Which car? Did it matter?

It did. I didn't want to go back to Laurel Canyon. I wanted my freedom. I wanted to get control of my life without Deacon's little rituals and rules. That was fake. It had all been fake. He'd put me in a straitjacket then complimented himself for keeping me still. Now I had to crawl into the straitjacket myself. I had to cruise downhill at my own speed, and with my own purpose. I had to be better, stronger, more regulated than even Deacon could make me.

I took the card, slapped the safe closed, then the cabinet, and walked to the outer room, where I caught a view of myself in one of the closet mirrors.

Who the hell was I kidding?

I peeled off my clothes as if they burned me, tossing them aside to look at myself naked.

Did he own this?

He'd laid claim to me a hundred times, and I'd relished it. Now suddenly, I didn't need that anymore? Only if he was right and I wasn't truly submissive. And if that were true, who was this woman?

My A-plus tits perked up from the cold. I rubbed them, and the pink nubs got rock hard.

Was I a freak?

With everything going on my life, all I could think about was sex.

Elliot's kiss had warmed me up, and pushing him away had turned me on, the disappointment sending my libido into a rage. And Deacon's paddling had left its wounds on my ass, which I saw when I sat on the carpet and spread my legs in front of the mirror. I saw the raw redness on the backs of my legs when I bent my knees, and I rubbed my hands along the wounds to make them hurt.

I made it last, stroking myself slowly, then quickly, watching myself in the mirror in a haze of pleasure. I wanted to see how long I could hold it back. How long I could delay my gratification.

And I imagined my safest place. Deacon knotting me up until I couldn't move, and Elliot taking me in his arms and putting his cock in me.

"Don't come. Don't—"

I pressed down harder, rubbing faster, gathering juice from my cunt to make my clit all the more slippery.

I felt the door opening behind me, and my eyes flew open. Behind me, in the mirror, stood Deacon.

I bit back shock and fear. Pushed away annoyance.

He didn't say a word as we stared at each other in the mirror. I didn't move my hand away from between my legs. He didn't break our gaze while he undid his belt and took out his dick. I still had the taste of it on my tongue.

"Who did it to you?" he asked.

"Did what?"

"Who raped you?"

Telling him was as good as killing Warren. Not a bad idea, on the whole, but it wasn't what I wanted for Deacon. I loved him. I wanted him to be safe from his own impulses, because he'd made me safe from mine.

"It wasn't rape."

"Put your hands on the mirror," he said as he kneeled behind me.

I swallowed. "Don't."

"Don't what? Take what belongs to me?" He lifted my hand and put it on the mirror.

"Not my ass. You don't have to reclaim it. Please. It wasn't Elliot."

His mouth tightened. "I didn't come for that." He pressed my lower back down and lifted my ass, running his fingers along the welts he'd made. "But your tone tells me more than your words."

He took a bottle of lotion from his pocket, and I almost wept. He'd paddled me, and we hadn't had any aftercare. No cuddling. No cathartic tears. No salve on my physical or emotional wounds.

He popped the top and squeezed a lump of lotion into his palm. It was my favorite. Vanilla-scented. I let my head fall into a relaxed position as the cool cream soothed my bottom.

"You're not submissive," he said.

I raised my head and watched him in the mirror as he carefully tended my bottom.

"I still mean it. When you're strong and safe, overall, you can be whatever you want. You're so complex. Deep and wide. I know there's no one like you, but you remind me of that constantly. You're not submissive unless you're weak from drugs, or needs, or a hurt you won't tell me about. Then you need it."

Gently, he pulled me up and gathered me in his arms.

This was wrong. I should not be accepting succor from Deacon after kissing Elliot. I was never so dishonest in my life as when I leaned into his chest and let him stroke my hair.

"You need a sub," I said.

"I do."

"I don't know what I need."

"You need to submit when you feel weak and not when you feel strong."

Was he right? Did my bad days just require a good paddling? Was he some kind of medicine for what ailed me? If he was right, then I couldn't leave him. I was done. Put a fork in me. I'd always be sick.

Given the choice between being a true submissive and someone who used submission to regulate herself, I wished for the real thing or nothing.

"You've done so much for me," I said. "I want you to know I'm grateful. But I'm confused right now."

"No." He was firm and Dominant again, as if I'd pulled a switch. "Someone's getting to you. I saw you in the car. He had his hands on what's mine." He turned my face to the mirror. "Look at yourself. This is mine. No one takes your ass without me there."

He pulled my legs apart, and the very act of showing him my cunt made me wet for him. My back arched for him. I ached for him to subjugate me. Was he right? Was that desire a key to my weakness when it should have been the key to my strength?

"You're my property until I release you."

"Yes." I agreed through all my questions. Habit. Need. Desire. The drug of Deacon Bruce.

He put his cock on my seam, sliding it from clit to bruised asshole. Every sensation went through my body, electric pleasure to sharp pain. He slid into me. First stroke down to the balls, pressing me down by the sternum. I stretched my arms over my head. I was still well-trained.

He put his thumb between my legs with his other hand. "No one hurts you unless I say." He ran circles around my clit. "No one. You're my property. When they hurt you, they offend me. And when you lie to me, Kitten…" He slammed his cock into me. "It offends me."

I was so caught up in pleasure I couldn't even speak. I came around him, sucking him into me. His hand moved constantly, and the orgasm went on forever, breaking me apart with pleasure. He came in me at the end of it, pushing me down on him.

He flipped me onto my stomach and put all his weight between my shoulder blades. I was pinned.

"Who took you?" He slid his free hand between my ass cheeks.

"No one."

He found my asshole, and with a finger wet from my cunt, he pressed forward, sliding the finger inside my ass.

I loved ass play, but this hurt in a way I hadn't experienced. The shredding was more emotional than physical. I smelled wet leaves and soil. Heard the dribbling of the creek behind Warren's delighted voice.

*Oh, you're so fucking tight for a slut.*

*I like it dry.*

*I'm going to get you for this.*

Deacon's breath on me, so close, watching my face as he slid in a second finger.

"This hurts you," he growled, taking his fingers out. "It shouldn't hurt. Who did it?"

"Take me, Master," I said with my face smushed into the carpet. "Fuck me in the ass."

I dared him to do it when he knew it wasn't what I wanted, because these were our roles. He did what he wanted to my body to exhibit his dominance. Usually, that worked out just fine for me, because it pushed my limits. But in my walk-in closet that day, it was I who pushed boundaries, and Deacon, like the Dominant he was, would not be pushed.

He got up on his knees. I leaned on my elbow, crying, face knotted in tight red tension. I swallowed a mess of tears and gunk, wiping my cheeks with my wrist.

He looked helpless, on his knees with his dick out. Abandoned by his most valuable skill, the ability to get what he wanted.

"Who are you protecting?" he demanded.

"You."

His face fell before the last vowel left my lips. I'd just turned his whole world upside down with a thoughtless and honest word. I would have been gentler if I'd realized what it would do to him, but after the orgasm and the emotional violence of it, I didn't have the brain power to lie.

"Me?" He asked it as if I'd shocked him so badly he had to repeat it to understand it.

"You."

I didn't know how to make him believe it. I didn't know how to make myself believe it either. But the words hung there, suspended between us, and to leave them unsaid was to lie about what we were.

"I don't think this is the right thing for me anymore," I finished. "I'm using you, and it's not right for either of us."

I couldn't look at him while the world slipped through his fingers. I got up and ran to the bathroom, locked the door, and turned on the shower.

Jesus Christ. What had I done? I looked at the shower knob too long, wondering what was next. Where I would go? Who would love me the way I needed to be loved? Would I spend the rest of my life in a state of free fall, doing everything I could to find out where the bottom was?

"I hear you on the other side of the door," I said. "I need you to just go. I'm not playing."

I got in the shower. By the time I'd scrubbed myself raw, he was gone. My apartment felt as big and lonely as five thousand square feet could, and I longed for company away from Deacon, away from Elliot, away from parties and drugs. Just company.

I scrolled through my phone and found Karen's number.

## chapter twenty-nine

FIONA

Karen's pool was inside a heated glass building. The roof retracted in the spring and fall, but in the summer, they just used the outdoor pool on the other side of the house. Her parents were gone. Her brothers were in school. The house was empty, as always. Her bikini was hooked around her hip bones, and she wore a huge T-shirt to cover imaginary fat. She smoothed it out so it didn't touch her skin. I wore a bikini top and shorts to cover the pink paddle marks.

"I used to want to be a fashion designer," she said. "I thought it would be so cool, you know. The runway shows. Getting girls all dressed up all the time. The parties."

"You could still do that."

"I'm too tired. I hear they actually work really hard." She bit her lip. "What do you want to do when you grow up?"

I was twenty-three years old, and I'd always wanted exactly what I had. Always been perfectly happy to be Fiona Drazen.

I said what I always said as if by rote. It all felt cold and hard in my mouth. "I want to be the girl all the paps want to shoot. The girl all the guys want to fuck. The girl who does what she wants. That's what everyone wants to be."

And it wasn't any more true by the pool than it had been in the weeks before Deacon showed me that what I wanted and needed were the same thing. Boundaries. Control. Rules. I'd been so happy to give myself to him, but I hadn't thought about what to do without him.

"You were always so happy with who you were," she said. "I hated you."

I laughed. "Sorry."

"Nah. It was me being jealous. Now I'm too tired to try to be you."

"Doesn't the IV drip help with that?" I popped my sunglasses to the top of my head.

"No," she said. "And I hate it. Even the stuff in the tube makes me feel full, and then it's like I can feel the fat getting on me."

It was no use telling her that she needed fat on her. I'd tried that. At the core of her being, she didn't believe it.

She laid back. "My nurse got me to take a bite of banana yesterday. I could feel it going down my throat. In my stomach. I felt dirty. It was like I was being invaded. No one gets it. I feel good when I'm hungry. I feel, I don't know, pure. Clean. It's the best feeling in the world. I'm not giving that up for a bite of banana."

"I guess I don't have to ask if you spit or swallow," I joked.

"Don't even get me started. Westonwood put me off men forever."

I froze, a million questions on my lips, but I knew asking any of them would only clam her up.

A few seconds later, after she put her head back and her face to the cold, glass-blocked sun, she spoke again. "Fucking Warren. I told him I wasn't taking his dick in my mouth. I said, specifically, no mouth. That stays clean. So what did he do? Fucker. I hate him."

"Shoulda bit it off." I said it as if it was nothing, but my heart was racing and my skin crawled.

"He got his buddy, what's his name…with the tattoos and the piercings he takes out? The orderly?"

"Mark."

"He held me down and pinched my nose. And Warren put his thing, like, way down. God, it was disgusting. I gagged, but I was empty. I had nothing to puke. He just kept putting it in me. His balls were on my lip. His literal gross balls. Ugh. And then when he came…I breathed and I said, 'Come on my face,' because I didn't want that shit inside me. But he shoved it back in and came down my throat. He held my mouth shut and made me swallow. And when Mark fucked me, he made him put me on my back so I couldn't puke it up."

She shook her head, and from under her sunglasses, a tear rolled along the side of her head.

"Karen, that's terrible."

"Whatever."

"Did you tell anyone?"

"Why? So he could tell them I got diet pills from him? I mean, seriously. It's not like I didn't fuck him willingly in Ojai, like, how many times? And his dad and my dad are, like, best friends from Overland. What's he going to do? Stop making Chilton movies? I don't think so. Whatever. I washed my mouth out with rubbing alcohol. It didn't kill me. I just won't go back there."

I didn't want to show her how upset I was, but my heart was racing. She weighed eighty pounds. Her voice was soft and raspy. I could rape her if I wanted. It was like torturing a small child.

"I'm going to pee," I said, standing. "You want something from inside? A tissue or something?"

"Sure."

I sat on the toilet in the pool house and buried my head in my hands, because I knew two things for certain: Karen was going back to Westonwood, and Warren was assaulting someone else every day.

The question was, what was I going to do about it?

I couldn't think straight. My body was crying out for sex. I wanted to get high, just a little high, so I could collect my thoughts. A line of flake would be fine. Just a line though. I couldn't get so fucked up I wouldn't be able to think.

But I knew there was no such thing as one line. I was a fuckup. I wasn't stupid.

If I went back to Deacon, I'd be in control. His control. So I'd be trapped.

Debbie. But she was inexorably tied with Deacon, and that meant she wasn't safe. She'd do whatever she thought was best for me.

Elliot.

Sure. He'd refer me to the proper authorities. That strategy was a loser from the gate. And he wouldn't fuck me, which chapped my hide.

It wasn't that hard. I had to figure it out. Maybe if I cleared my head, I'd wake up with a plan to get Elliot to…I didn't know. Get Deacon into Westonwood to remove Warren's asshole?

Even as I snapped tissues out of the dispenser, I knew I was lying to myself. I knew the old head-clearing methods didn't work. I knew I'd wake up useless. I'd go back to the old ways. Elliot would notice and then….

And then. Right.

Karen was dry-eyed when she took the tissues and left a dense pack of sand in my soul. I felt as if I'd abandoned the world to Warren Chilton, yet a heaviness filled me. Things had to be done. I didn't know what. I didn't know how. But a Fiona with an emotionless voice told me that this couldn't continue. She surprised me with her gravitas and her dominance over the constant questions that circled my thoughts.

*You will make this stop.*

And there it was. For what it was worth, it brought a peace to my heart.

"I'm hungry," I said. "I think everyone's going to The Thing later. Wanna come? They have water."

She shrugged, not getting my joke. "Sure."

"I have someone to meet now. See you there later."

## chapter thirty

FIONA

Behind the Westonwood campus, on the shoulder of a two-lane blacktop with the electrified fence fifty feet away through trees and brush, I decided to let it go. My hands clenched the bottom of the steering wheel and my jaw hurt from my teeth grinding, but I could let it go.

I got out of the car.

I didn't know what I expected to see, or what I wanted, but I walked through the trees to the fence. Yellow-and-black signs warned against contact, and along the length of the chain link, over fallen needles and broken sandy earth, I came to the creek, and the tree, and the place where he'd raped me.

If I was giving up on going back, I was giving up on ever mentioning what had happened. No one would believe me. I was a whore. I spread myself open for anyone who could handle me.

I touched the chain link.

The shock was mild. Barely even painful.

*Really?* I'd thought I would get thrown back ten feet.

I curled my fingers around the diamond-twisted wires and looked in. The bones of my hand rattled and itched. My elbows tingled. I took my hand away. That hurt.

Under that tree, where Deacon had given me back my memory and Warren had taken what he wanted, the creek gurgled and the leaves rustled in the breeze. The tree didn't give a shit. It would go on as if nothing had ever happened.

Margie's car came up the twisted forest road, just below the legal speed limit. I was already leaning on my car. I'd been early. My sister was on time.

My ass would stop hurting. My ego would heal. I was back in the safety of the world.

Could I let it go?

Warren didn't have to be a problem if I didn't want him to be.

I let go of the fence.

"Bitch," I said, pointing at the spot, "I am not a tree."

I'd told Margie what had happened with Warren. It was less painful in the second telling, and the listener didn't want to fuck me, which was also nice. Of course she wanted to "do something," so I told her I was going to the scene of the crime if she wanted to join me for a little fun.

Margie stopped right behind my car. She seemed to take forever to get out. Me, I just turned off the ignition and got out of the car. She seemed to have a list of tasks. Roll up windows. Turn off radio. Dick with some settings I couldn't see. Put up visor. Slide folder under seat. Place keys in bag. Pick up bag. Get out.

"Where's the body?" She tried to hug me, but I turned away.

"He's not dead," I said. "He's still behind a bunch of walls."

"Sister," she said, "I thought you had him killed or something when you told me to meet you here. After that story."

"I don't know what I want out of you, exactly. I wanted to show you the place because…I don't know why. You'd know I was telling the truth if you saw it, which is ridic. It's just a patch of nothing land."

"You thought I wouldn't believe you?"

"You wouldn't believe I said no."

She leaned next to me, arms crossed, Hermes bag hanging. "I believe you. More than believe you. I'm angry and hurt for you. I have a plan for how to bring charges without—"

"No!"

"What do you mean 'no'? I can protect you."

"God, you're as bad as Elliot. Think about it. Charlie Chilton's oldest child. More money than the government, and more power too. Do you think he's going to Soledad? No. They'll cop a plea to a psych ward, and here he stays."

"They'll only cop a plea if the prosecution offers. If we don't offer it, he goes to trial."

"And?"

"And we nail him."

"You're such an optimist," I mumbled.

She shook her head and stared at the fenced-in area behind the facility. "Did you tell your therapist?"

"Yes." I didn't elaborate.

"He has to report it."

"Isn't there some kind of privilege?"

"Not when the law's broken." She pushed off the car and faced me. "I can't let this sit. It's rotting my stomach. Since you told me, all I can think about is helping you. I have a corporate client messaging me right now about three million in a Burmese account he can't access because of a subpoena, and I don't even care. All I care about is making this right for you."

"Okay, wait—"

"We may have different idea about right—"

"No, no, no. Stop." I had my hands up, and she clapped her mouth shut. "I'm the only one who can make this right for me."

"You're not an island."

"Yes, I am. We all are. We have to manage our own shit. We can't put it on other people."

"Okay then. You're an island in an archipelago. I'm the island right next to you, and I'm here for you. I'm going to pressure you to go through all the legal channels available to you."

I shook my head. "I wanted to meet you so you'd talk me into that. Didn't work, you know. I still feel like it's pointless."

"I'm your lifeline to reality. Don't hold on to this forever."

"I'll think about it, okay?"

My sister nodded and held me as a mother should. If she didn't talk me into it on that day, she would soon enough. Unless Elliot had told already.

## chapter thirty-one

FIONA

"We can't go back to this," Elliot said, leaning back in his chair.

His office at Alondra was the exact opposite of his office at Westonwood. Here in Compton, he had a plastic office chair with worn grey fabric on the back, a desk with enough folders to hold back a tsunami, and white horizontal blinds with a dusting of black soot. The window overlooked a parking lot.

"Back?" I said from the chair across from him. "I don't want to go back. I want to go forward. I don't have anyone else. And I trust you."

He pivoted his pen half a quarter inch from the top, then spun it ninety degrees. "I can't go back to sitting on this side of a desk from you anymore. I have to listen and be objective, and I'm not objective anymore." He fussed with the pen again.

"I'm really trying to keep my shit together," I said with a cracked voice.

"Me too." He rocked back in his chair, moved his pen over, then snapped it up and thrust it into a cup. "I want to hear it. I want you to talk to me. But I'm not safe anymore. I want to tell you that up-front. I can't look at you from a distance."

"I'm just going through the day, and I either feel nothing or I want to break stuff. And honestly, I prefer the feeling of wanting to break stuff. So, safe. Not safe. Whatever."

His face was so tender, so compassionate and real, that I wanted to fall into its warmth. He looked at his watch. "Let's go for a walk."

***

My shoes cost something like twelve hundred dollars. I could have thrown them in the trash and forgotten what they looked like before I even got home. The couple two benches down didn't seem to mind the fast food garbage everywhere, or the graffiti, or the patches of brown grass. If the lingering background scent of urine bothered them, I'd never know. I'd stopped smelling it when he brushed his fingers along the back of my neck.

"Once it's out, they're going to talk about my past. And I want you to know I'll never apologize for it. Never. I lived the way I wanted. I may or may not change that. It's my choice."

He smiled and looked down as if trying to hide it. I ignored the smirk. I wasn't done.

"And you're going to hear about it. You're going to know. Men and women are going to come out of the woodwork, and guess what? I'm not denying one goddamn orgy."

A laugh shot out of him as if it wouldn't be contained.

"What?"

"I love how you are." He put his hand over mine. "And I'm not being sarcastic. I love how you're not ashamed of what you chose."

"Well, yeah, I have plenty of shame. About things I lied about, and when I hurt people. I'm not happy about that stuff. But, all right, moving on."

"Moving on," he said into my cheek. "What do you want to do?"

His lips pressed on my skin. I leaned into him.

"I want you to do whatever you'd do if a patient told you she was raped by the creek."

"Administrator, then law enforcement."

"My sister Margie's going to the cops. She's a lawyer."

"I think this is the right thing. Are you ready though?"

"No. But let's do it anyway. I mean, it's a waste of time in a way. But since he's getting out, I think the world needs to know. I think Westonwood made him bold. If I don't say something, he's going to get out and use Los Angeles as a bigger hunting ground."

"Jail is a tough hunting ground."

"He's not going to jail. The most that'll happen? I'll be the least popular girl at all the parties, but hopefully it'll keep people from being alone in a room with him."

"I think it'll go better than you think."

I didn't have such high hopes. .

"I left Deacon."

"I figured."

"How do you figure?" Maybe I was defensive. I had the right to be. Since when was I so predictable?

And was he assuming I'd left for him? Because I hadn't, and I was about to run to my own defense when he leaned back, spread his legs and arms over the bench, and took in the view of the Compton park. He bounced one foot a couple of times.

"We break down and rebuild ourselves every seven to ten years. He built the last Fiona. But now you're rebuilding yourself, and he's just going to try to stop you." He turned back to me, and his smirk made me want to slap him and kiss him, in that order. "You didn't invent this."

"Why are you sitting here with me if I'm so predictable?"

"You walked into my office and demanded to see me."

"Fine. My bad." I got up and walked. I didn't know what direction I was walking in, but I'd figure it out.

Of course he came after me.

Of course he grabbed my arm and pulled me to him.

It wasn't like he was inventing this either.

"If you hadn't come, I would have found you."

"Then what? I'm not your project. I'm a girl you want to fuck. So instead of just saying to yourself, 'I want to fuck her,' you made up this line of bullshit about saving me from Deacon, from myself, from everything. What are you going to lose to make excuses for your dick? Huh? You already lost the girlfriend. You're this close to losing your job. All that for a fuck? Yeah, I get why you have to make up big reasons about rebuilding yourself. I get it. But let's do this instead." I stepped toward him until my chest was an inch from his and I had to tilt my head back to face him. "Let's just fuck. You don't have to save me. You don't have to pretend you love me. You. Just. Fuck."

"Fiona..." His voice was low and soft.

"Scared?"

"Come on."

"Afraid you might not measure up?"

He smiled. "I measure up."

"Then what are you scared of?"

"Nothing, just—"

"*Bok bok bok.*"

"You daring me?"

"I'm daring you to let me blow your mind. Nothing more. Nothing less. I'm daring you to stop trying to save me. Just take what you want without all the baggage."

"What's in it for you?" he asked.

"Getting you off my back."

"Really?"

"Really."

He stepped away and looked off into the smoggy horizon, a little smile on his face. I had my reasons for wanting to sleep with him, not the least of which was the fact that I liked him. A lot. I liked the way he spoke and the things he said. I liked his openness and vulnerability. He had beautiful hands, and deep inside him was a sexuality I wanted to experience.

But, yeah, the reasons.

"Let's do it," I said. "It'll be fun."

"Fun?"

"Yeah. Not too many men can resist a night with me."

"I'm not too many men. I'm one man. And when I have you, Fiona, I'll be sacrificing my career. So when I finally take you to bed, I won't be changing my life for a little pussy. I'm changing it for a woman."

"If you wait, doctor, I might not be around when you're ready."

"You'll wait."

He was right. I would. I'd changed in Westonwood. Partly it was Elliot. Partly it was Warren. And partly, well, who knew? But I was going to wait because I had the feeling he'd be worth it.

## chapter thirty-two

FIONA

The Thing existed for people exactly like me and was closed to gapers and hangers-on. No reservations required, but it was still the hardest meal to get in Los Angeles, unless you were me.

The second-floor dining room was accessed through the restaurant kitchen and up a narrow flight of stairs, where a man waited. His name was Diego, and he was a star. If he knew your face, you were in. If he didn't, you could go eat downstairs or go home. Not his problem.

Once you got through the door, the space opened up like a whore's legs. Two floors and fifteen thousand square feet. Windows that let the street see that something was happening up there, even if it was inaccessible.

The rectangular tables were set in a herringbone up and down the huge space, and everything was glow-in-the-dark white. Literally. The lights were shut for ten minutes every hour, and the tables, plates, and wall designs became visible in glowing green.

One dish was served to everyone. The Thing wasn't about the food.

I waved to Baby and Mindy in the back and made my way across the floor. Karen leaned on me. Arrow waved. I could tell from across the room he was jacked.

"Hey!" Baby cried, kissing my cheek. I could smell her makeup. "We were just talking about your brother."

"Jonathan?"

A plate with food appeared in front of me. Karen waved hers away.

"The one and only," Baby said, shifting the hump of beef stew around his enormous plate. "He's making my brother nuts. Won't take pills. Wants booze, the one thing Warren can't get in."

"You guys!" Mindy laughed. "You all are so crazy!" Her pupils were vinyl records with blue pencil around them.

"Jonathan's fucking with him," I said. "He's not a user."

"Oh, he uses," Baby said. "Uses that dick. It's famous."

"And the hands," Mindy added. "I had bruises for a week." She bit her lower lip.

By the look on her face, I was forced to imagine things I didn't want to imagine. She was twenty-six, and my brother was not in her fucking age group. But that didn't matter. Not a bit. Maybe in a different universe her comment would have stirred some emotion in me, but in mine, I was supposed to chuckle and blow it off. The conversation continued around other matters of no importance, and I seethed. I was sober. That was the problem. And the glass of wine I sat sipping did nothing to bring me to the plane of jacked-up silliness these people took so seriously. I was an outsider.

"That's my brother, bitch," I said too late and too loud. "He's six-fucking-teen."

The table dropped into silence.

"Go do a line, Fiona," Baby said. "You're being a drag."

Had she fucked my brother? And why did I care? He was a big boy. I knew he was sexually active with Rachel at the very least. He could decide what to do with his dick, though

I didn't want to picture it, ever. Period. But for some reason, the thought of Baby fucking him was about to put me over the edge, even without imagining the act itself. Something about it being Baby Chilton.

The lights dropped, and the room exploded in glowing green shapes. The dim echo of conversation went on, and I bit my lip before I could speak.

*Why aren't you letting yourself think the obvious?*

*Is it because you love your brother?*

*Why isn't that comfortable for you?*

Elliot's voice warmed me. Calmed me. With the lights out, I was back in his office under hypnosis.

*Use different words to describe yourself.*

*Loyal.*

*Protective.*

*Capable of love.*

I was uncomfortable. Emotionally out of sorts. A line of flake would have fixed that nicely, but I wanted to sit inside the discomfort and understand it. More proof I was crazy. But the ten minutes of dark was the perfect time to stare inward and observe the tangle, and the titter of my friends' voices was the perfect sound to back up against. I was another stroke in a larger painting, and even my discomfort over my brother's initiation into my sick life seemed like the right pigment.

Which didn't mean I was letting Jonathan make my mistakes. Once he was out—

The lights went on, and though nothing significant had changed for anyone else, two things had changed for me.

One, a tiny shift in my perception of myself and my ability to change the lives of people I loved.

Two, Deacon stood across from me.

Baby was looking at him like she wanted to eat him alive.

"Fiona," he said as if stating a fact.

I crossed my arms. I wasn't doing anything I should be ashamed of, and not because he hadn't given me permission to snort shit or whatever, but because I didn't want to. Because I'd come to The Thing looking for food and companionship.

"Deacon." I stood.

"Oh hey," purred Mindy. "I remember you! I—"

"I'm bringing you back to Laurel Canyon." His eyes never left mine.

For a second, I thought that was what I wanted. To be lost in the sharp calm of his world, where everything could be predicted and what was unplanned had a response.

I opened my mouth to tell him I wasn't doing anything wrong. I was clean. I was just eating and having a glass of wine. I wasn't even driving home. But I snapped my jaw shut.

*You are a grown woman.*

And he was just another drug.

## chapter thirty-three

FIONA

*Why do you want to know?*

*I've been with Deacon a long time, and you never said anything about that. Was it because there was a connection with us? You and me?*

*I can't see my own connections.*

*So?*

*So.*

*Debbie, are you going to answer my question?*

We had to cross a fake cobblestone lane to get to the parking lot. I'd taken a cab. Deacon drove. So we had to exit and cross, and I didn't even know if I wanted to go with him.

The paps waited outside in a pack. I'd be in the news with Deacon's hand on my back. They didn't faze him, no matter what they said. One time, early in our relationship, a pap had tried to get a rise out of him by calling me Deacon's Famous Little Fucktoy.

I thought he'd fly off the handle, but he didn't. He stared at the man, and the pap never came around again. After that, they didn't say much to me when he was around, unless they were new. Another stare, and it was done.

We walked into the lot.

A valet approached, and Deacon waved him off. "I'll get it myself."

We took the stairs, as always. No elevator. No one handles the car but him.

So many little things.

Like the way he walked a little bit behind me. The way he opened a door slowly and didn't go through right away, or the way he checked right then left before he let me walk through it first. The casual spot check of the car. The way he unlocked it from as far away as possible then locked it again so if it exploded, we were half a garage away.

I stopped and pressed my fingers to my eyelids. "I can't do this." My voice echoed in the empty concrete space.

"Then *what?*" he shouted.

He never shouted.

"I'm just using you. Don't you see that?"

"What do you want?" His jaw tightened. He pointed the key at me as if he were going to unlock me remotely with a light-flashing beep.

"I want to be normal."

"Jesus Christ. You might as well want to be taller. Normal wasn't the hand you were dealt. You and I, we're not normal. That's not a choice we have."

"I know. I..."

I stopped myself. Did I want to do this? Out here in the parking lot, with the sound of tires screeching around turns somewhere in the depths, did I want to do this? I'd done an incomplete job in my penthouse if he thought he could just show up.

"You were supposed to be away," I said. "On the continent. Why did you stay?"

"Africa's just one fucking crisis after another. But you? You're broken, and if I'm not here to fix it, I'm responsible for what happens."

"Okay, listen to me. You aren't responsible for my shit. You know who's responsible for that? Me. All me. I've been putting myself in stupid situations. I've been fucking crazy. And it's my fault. Not yours. Everything that happens is my fault." I took a deep breath. "That's not true. Not everything is my fault, but the stuff I choose? That's mine. Yes, I put myself in a ton of shit this week, and yes, I got out of all of it. I think I was testing myself. But also..." I swallowed. My spit tasted like metal.

"Also?"

He brushed my forearm, his fingers landing in the curve of my palm. It was so easy to fall into him and just submit myself. I pulled my hand away.

"Don't. I can't use you anymore. And I can't treat you like a barometer. Or whatever. I don't even know what a barometer does. But if it's something a grown woman looks at to decide if she's doing right or wrong, then I can't use you for that."

"This is what it is. And if it works? What's the problem?"

"It doesn't work. I didn't tell you who hurt me in Westonwood because you'd freak out and kill someone."

He raised his finger. "I knew it—"

"You don't know anything."

"I saw what he did."

"I'm the only one who can make it right. I'm the only one who can stop it from happening to someone else. I just..." As if the underground parking lot had cracked open and sunlight shone through, I knew the problem. "I was scared. I thought if I brought it up, I'd be asking the universe for it to happen again."

He put his hands on my jaw and moved his face close to mine. I didn't feel safe or enclosed, but I didn't feel endangered. I felt a responsibility to him, as a man, as a lover, as a friend who cared about me.

"What happened?" he said in a low voice, not his Dominant tone, but something just as serious.

"Right before I left, I went to the creek with him to talk about the sleeping pills he got me. He raped me. It hurt. I told him to stop. But I had to get out of there, so I didn't tell anyone."

"You sat next to me in my car right after he did that?"

I nodded, looking down. "I wasn't trying to shut you out."

"Who was it?"

"Doesn't matter." I looked into his eyes. "I'm going to take care of it."

"I can't tell you what it does to me that someone hurt you. You're mine. I chose you. To not go there and kill him right now…where I'm from, I'd tie him to the back of my Jeep and drag him through the street until he didn't have a bone left that wasn't broken."

"To send a message."

"To make you feel safe. I have no tools here. Anyone can take what's mine, and I can't do anything."

"I have tools. But I can't drag him around the street. This isn't Africa."

"Let me help you then."

I pressed my lips together. "This is going public. You can help me by not getting mad about it. You should probably go back to Johannesburg, because your privacy is probably going to be not-so-private anymore."

He leaned on one foot, the picture of male perfection. His presence in the ugly parking lot made it more beautiful, yet he looked at a complete loss. "I don't know what I care about besides you."

I took a deep breath, because I had to expand my chest to fit a new love for him. I'd never known why he needed me, and with those words, I understood it all. By sheltering the unprotectable, controlling the out-of-control, he gave himself a task so impossible, he'd never run out of shit to keep him from his own problems.

I loved him more than ever.

I took his cheeks in my hands.

"I'm going home, Master."

## chapter thirty-four

FIONA

I dreamed dreams of a narrow wall reaching to the sky. I walked on the top, toe to heel. Then with wider strides, and wider, until I was running, fearlessly, recklessly, Los Angeles beneath me at cruising altitude. The wall ended, and I walked on the sky. Then I feared, and fell, and woke to another day.

I had a voice mail from Elliot when I got out of the shower.

*I want you to know. I told the admins. They're investigating. You're going to be fine, no matter what. And I'm here for you, no matter what.*

My lungs got too small for breaths. I nearly choked on my own spit. People were going to know. They'd talk about how I'd said no. They'd come and ask me about it. I sat on the bathroom floor, wet and naked, staring at his message.

The phone rang.

"Fiona?" Elliot asked. "Are you all right?"

"Yes."

"Your sister already told law enforcement. They came right after. They want to do an examination."

I didn't answer.

"Fiona?"

"I'm not a victim."

"You don't have to use that word."

"They will."

"You're not alone. I'm here. If you can't lean on me, I talked to your sister. She'll be there for you every step—"

I hung up. Half a second later, the screen lit up with Margie's name.

It was all over.

## chapter thirty-five

FIONA

The rape kit was as bad as I thought it would be, and it was probably for nothing, because it had been days since the assault. But the woman from LAPD insisted it could only help. After the first two hours, the speculum, the swabs, the photographs of my ass, we hadn't even started.

"There's no point," Margie said from behind me. I was in stirrups, and the young tech was coming at me with tape. "We have to skip combing for hair. She's showered."

"We can skip anything you want."

"No," I said. "If we're doing it, we're doing it."

Margie squeezed my hand through the exam.

Afterward, we sat at a desk and I described everything in brutal, painful detail to a female detective in a button down shirt. She seemed more angry about it than I did, and I appreciated that. Margie was the most irritated. I felt her anger at the process. It radiated through her tan suit in the form of a calm, dead heat.

"It's okay," I said in the cafeteria when the detective had been called away. Margie needed more comfort than I did.

My phone rang. Elliot again. I shut it. He wanted to be there, and I didn't want him anywhere near me. Not for this.

"Daddy's going to find out," she said.

"He's not going to believe me."

A shadow passed over us, and I looked up to find out who had blocked the light.

"Speak of the devil," Margie said.

"And he shall appear, Margaret."

Our father wore a perfect suit and held his hands in front of him as if he didn't want to appear too threatening. It didn't work. The full head of sandy-red hair came to a point at the center, reminding me that maybe I shouldn't speak of him if I didn't want him to show up.

"Where's Mom?" I asked.

"Ibiza. I told her to stay. I have this." He turned his sharp eyes to Margie. "Will you excuse us?"

"She's going to tell me everything anyway. So no."

Margie, of all of us, was the least afraid of Declan Drazen.

He swung a chair around and sat with us. He stared at me as if I had a really good book stuck to my face.

"What?" I asked.

"You're telling the truth?"

"Dad," Margie protested.

He ignored her.

"Of course I'm telling the truth."

"May I be frank and less than politically correct?" he asked.

"No," Margie said, but she was ignored again.

"Go the fuck ahead. I don't care."

"Your reputation precedes you. It's an ugly thing to say, but how you act affects how people treat you. You don't have to like it. It's the world."

"Really?" Margie looked ready to jump out of her skin. "Are you fucking with her?"

I pointed at him and spoke firmly. "I said no. No is no, regardless of how many guys fucked me this year or this week." I spat it out, hoping to upset him. I failed.

"I know. And for that, I'm going to destroy him and the family that created him. That kid's always been trouble, and they allowed it. I can't abide anyone knowing they took what wasn't theirs. That they took it *from us.* But that's why I need to make sure you're telling the truth and this isn't some game."

"You're sick if you think I'd play a game like this."

"Maybe. I'm guilty of plenty. Your mother too. The number one mistake we made was raising you the same way Warren was raised, and we're setting it right."

"You going to unraise her, Dad?" Margie's arms were crossed so tight, it looked as if she had one sleeve around both forearms.

"It's time you took some responsibility." He sat up straight. "I warned you this could happen if you slipped again, and you did. In Holmby Hills. We heard all about it. You can keep your non-liquid assets, but the trust is revocable. We're exercising our right to remove you until further notice. I'm sorry, Fiona. It's for the best."

"Miss Drazen?" The detective came back and leaned over the table. "Do you want to finish?"

I stood. "Yes. I'll finish." I turned to Dad. "You can take the money. I get your logic. It's stupid and too late, but I get it. Now fuck off. And thank Mom for coming by."

I threw up a middle finger and followed the detective to the back without seeing how Dad reacted.

## chapter thirty-six

FIONA

"How did it go?" Elliot asked from his doorway. Pajama bottoms. No shirt. Beautiful. He was better toned than I ever expected from a psychologist trained for the priesthood. And with his hair mussed from sleep and the scruff on his chin, I found myself attracted to him as if I hadn't been before. And I had been, but I'd been attracted to him as a person. I wanted to fuck him because of who he was, but standing in the doorway, I wanted him because he was physically beautiful in his bafflement.

"Terrible. Yesterday was the worst day of my life. I should have just hired someone to murder him."

Elliot didn't have blood in his revenge fantasies. He dreamed of justice and goodness. I wished I could be like him. I admired his squeaky-clean soul. His commitment to *rightness*. And there I was at five in the morning, like a devil on his shoulder.

"But it's kind of a relief. Like a weight's off."

"Come in," he said, stepping out of the way. "You can tell me all about how you'd murder him."

The house was dark. He'd gone to the door without turning on a light, and I wanted to see it. All of it. Would the house be as warm as his office? Would the rug and chair be inviting? Would the light ask gentle questions?

"Can I make you tea or something?" he asked.

"Do you have coffee?"

"No."

"Tea is fine." I could see the kitchen from where I stood. "I'll make it."

"Sit. I have it. Just give me a minute to clear the crap out of my eyes."

He padded down a short hall and into the bedroom. A soft light came from it. I wanted to see inside.

What the hell was wrong with me?

Was I nervous? I didn't get nervous. Not around men. Not around anyone I wanted to fuck. I was in charge.

I clicked a switch over the toaster. Cold light flooded the surfaces: the granite countertop, the tiles, the grain in the wood cabinets. I snapped the teapot off the stove and filled it. I didn't even like tea. Fuck this.

I put the teapot on the burner. *Click click click.* The stove wouldn't light.

Fuck this again. I'd waited all night, staring at the ceiling, debating whether to come see him or not, only to stand here unable to light the fucking stove.

The room light went from cold blue fluorescent to warm and dim with a click. With a *whoosh,* the burner flamed blue.

Elliot leaned in the doorway, hair straightened, T-shirt covering the body I'd just admired.

"Thanks," I said, taking my eyes off him. I should have just grabbed his dick. Nothing like a straight line between two points. But I didn't know what would go over with this guy, if anything. I was probably going to chase him all over LA and wind up turned away. "I like the incandescent light too."

"We have something in common. We need to write that down."

I wished the water to boil, which never worked. It just did its thing, and Elliot just waited. Goddamn him and his patience.

"I have a fantasy," I said.

"I'd love to hear it."

"As my therapist? Or my friend?"

"As your…I don't know what we are." He smiled as if it was funny. As if he was the relaxed one in the room. I was the wreck, and he was just fine with uncertainty.

My little dreams of revenge had never left my lips, and on the tip of my tongue, each one was, by varying degrees, embarrassing, shameful, painful, and very likely to make him hate me.

"I imagine I have a broom handle," I said, watching that stupid, inefficient teapot do nothing, "and I put a nail in it. I bend the head toward me, so it goes in his ass smooth and rips him up when I pull it out."

He didn't seem shocked or put off, so I continued.

"The rest involve his balls. And one where I give him a boner and tie off his dick until his erection turns purple. Then I just, you know, leave it for days."

"Making your dreams come true is going to require a whole serial killer setup."

I laughed and he smiled, looking at me with those grey-green eyes. I was smaller, more vulnerable, and somehow safer in that little joke, because it was said without passion or judgment.

"I thought you'd think I was sick," I said.

The teapot hissed but didn't boil.

He stepped into the kitchen and leaned on the counter. "There's this drug. It's called Nortyl. It's used for bipolar patients to manage manic episodes, and only under strict supervision. It brings them back down to earth. Helps. Really helps. But if the dose is too strong, it creates a feeling of utter despair. The psychic pain can be unbearable. They'll be terrified, but only have the feeling of terror, because there's nothing to be afraid of. No object. Just the feeling. The patient won't die from an overdose, but they will commit suicide if you don't catch them in time. I had one girl get her hands on a bunch and try to OD on it. We had to tie her down. She banged her head on the back of the chair until we tied that down too. She compared the feeling to her soul being ripped to shreds. She used words like desolation. Misery. Grief so deep she was in hell. Just the feeling, no reason for it." He took two cups and teabags from the cabinet as if he needed to keep his body moving. "When you told me what he did to you, I wondered, really wondered…could I arrange sixty milligrams? Maybe fifty would do it, but seventy would be optimum. God, a hundred milligrams would rip a person apart emotionally. And he's in a mental ward already, so he'd be tied down. Wouldn't even hurt him really. Not physically." He turned each cup a quarter turn until both handles faced him, and he stared into the empty cups as if an answer sat at the bottom of them. "For the last few days, doing it seemed not just possible, but sane."

The teapot whistled.

"I'm not the man I thought I was." He leaned over and shut off the burner. "I see him talking to your brother, and I can see he's fine. He doesn't even think about it. I start considering the Nortyl." He poured the water.

"I thought you were going to tell me to forgive him," I said.

He handed me the mug. It was warm against my palm.

"I ain't Jesus. I'm just a man."

"This whole thing got out of my hands yesterday."

"It's about the system, not you anymore."

I held the cup to my chin and looked over the edge at him. "I had no idea until yesterday, when I told the story the hundredth time. He thinks he's God, making trades and changing the rules."

"God doesn't make trades. He giveth and he taketh away. Period."

I nodded. Sure. It wasn't like I knew shit about theology. He took the cup from me and put his next to mine on the counter.

Then he kissed me.

He'd kissed me before. This was different. This was an invasion. His mouth, his tongue, the taste of toothpaste and tea. I put my hips on his, pushing against his erection, clutching him. He pulled back, lips popping when we separated.

"Yes," I said. "Yes."

He took a breath through his teeth. "I'm not a casual fuck."

"Neither am I. Not with you."

He put his hand between my legs, four fingers curling into me, the texture of my clothes a hot friction. I gasped.

"Are you wet?"

"Yes."

There was a moment as he looked at me when he had a second thought. It was all over his face. The ethics. The impropriety. The risk to his heart. I saw all of it come, and I watched all of it drop off him.

"Show me," he said.

I stuck my hand down my pants and touched myself. My clit was swollen with the possibility of him. Finally. I threw my head back it was so sensitive.

"Now, Fiona. Now."

I took my hand out and put my finger to his lips. He took it in his mouth and sucked off my juice.

"God forgive me," he said and dropped to his knees. "You taste like heaven."

He slipped my pants down and put his lips between my legs. He opened them and draped one knee over his shoulder. He kissed my clit, groaning.

This was it. All those weeks of talking across a desk. Watching his hands fidget, his lips move, the color of his eyes—the greyish-green the ocean actually was, not the way it was imagined. His voice behind me in the depths of hypnosis, and now his tongue flicking the wet skin between my legs. Those hands not fidgeting but moving up my body and grabbing my nipples, unafraid of the pain in the twist.

"Yes. Hurt them. Yes."

His stubble dug into the sensitive skin of my inner thigh when he opened his mouth to put his tongue inside me. I tugged his hair, and he slowed his mouth then stopped, leaving only the painful tug on my nipples.

"Do you want to come?"

"Yes."

"Beg for it." He ran the very tip of his tongue along the edge of my clit. He was going to drive me insane.

"Please, Elliot."

He pulled away. Paused. Set his jaw.

"Turn around. Hands on the counter." He raised an eyebrow, and a little smile played over his lips.

It was my turn to pause. Elliot wasn't Deacon. He meant it, but playfully. I put my chest to the counter.

I had no idea what to expect when he drew his hand down my back and over my ass. It went away then came down hard with a *smack*. I gasped with surprise. I couldn't see him, but he might have gasped as well.

"This is for being a tease." He slapped me twice more. Hard enough to sting. Hard enough to make my skin feel alive. "No. It's not. It's just because I want to."

He spanked me again, laying them quickly over each cheek, then he slid his fingers between, feeling how wet I was. I made a sharp vowel sound, and he was a little more articulate.

"Wow."

I shot out a laugh, and so did he.

"First time?" I asked over my shoulder.

"Not the last."

I sucked air through my teeth, breathing in the promise of it, and he leaned down to look me in the eye, then hit me again.

I groaned and whispered, "Harder."

He grabbed a handful of hair on the back of my head and tightened his fist while pressing me down until I couldn't move. The rain of open-handed blows stung, and I tried to wiggle away, but he held me still, moving unexpectedly to the backs of my thighs.

Two fingers, right inside, down to the webs of his hands.

I didn't have to be silent. What a relief to just say it.

"Fuck me," I growled. "Please. God. Just fuck me."

"Not yet."

He leaned down and put his tongue to the sore part of my ass, raising the sting in loops, then compressing the flesh and biting it.

"First, you come for me."

He bit the sore spot where my butt met my thigh, a new sort of pain awakening me. He opened the skin of my thighs, exposing my cunt to his tongue. He was rough with his fingers and gentle with his mouth, sucking on my clit while his fingers moved inside me.

"Elliot," I squeaked. "Please. Let me. I want to come so hard for you."

He reduced the pressure just a touch but kept moving consistently, so when I did shudder for him, tightening my muscles around his fingers and exploding in his mouth, the orgasm lasted until I felt boneless. My orgasm was defiance and surrender. Fuck him. Fuck the world for saying I couldn't have him. He owned me with his gentleness and roughness. This fucking fuck. I was his.

He pulled me onto the floor and got on top of me, wedging himself between my legs. I reached for his pants, but he slapped my hand away and got out his own damn dick.

"I haven't fucked anyone in my life as hard as I'm going to fuck you right now."

"I love it when you—"

I never finished the thought because he put his cock in me, sliding in against the slickness of my juice and his spit, and my words turned into a single groaning sound.

He fucked me as hard as he'd promised, but slower than I'd expected, letting each thrust explode into pleasure, fade, then rise again. I put my hands on his face, because I couldn't believe how beautiful he was, but he ripped them away and pinned them over my head. His thrusts picked up speed, driving deep, his body pressing against me with each stroke.

"I'm…God…" I gasped. "Again, I'm going to come again."

"Yes. You are. With. Me."

"Say when. Tell—"

"Now. Now, Fiona."

I saw the first seconds of his orgasm. His face went red, stiffening and slackening at the same time. I'd done that. I'd brought him there. He was mine. And with that thought, I said his name and exploded around him.

We slowed our rhythm, kissing the remnants of our pleasure away.

## chapter thirty-seven

ELLIOT

Freud defined three strata of the unconscious. They battle constantly. The animal instinct that wants to hurt, to fuck, to eat and shit. The higher self that want to love, to keep peace, to do right, to live in society. And the director that manages the two actors, letting the animal out when food was necessary and the conscience out when cooperation was necessary.

Mostly, the referee shuts the two factions backstage so the subject can function.

But the battle rages where it can't be seen, and when the ego is weakened, the victor steps out from behind the curtain and pulls levers and switches.

I brought her back to my bedroom and took her again and again. She became vulnerable before me, opening herself and letting me own her until I lost myself and became a beast.

Without her armor, she was more beautiful than I'd imagined possible. In her sleep, lids fluttering, lashes glowing copper in the morning light, I loved her. I just did. When she cringed in her sleep and whispered, "No, stop. It hurts. No," and her eyes squeezed tight against a remembered pain, a need to jump from the bed and take action cut through me.

For too long a war had been raging behind the scenes. A war between a physical need for her and an intellectual need to detach myself from her. Fucking her tore the curtain down, ripped it to shreds, and burned the theater to cinders.

The director was gutted.

In the wreckage stood an animal.

I was willing to do whatever it took to keep her from that pain again. He'd marked her with it, and I wanted to take that away.

When she flipped onto her stomach, I drew my hand over her back and down her ass, feeling the depth of the seam between.

She sighed and opened her eyes. "Good morning again."

I got on top of her, hard again, and kissed her shoulders and the back of her neck. "Good morning." I put my hands under her waist and pulled up her hips. "On your knees, please."

She stuck out her ass. I pushed down between her shoulder blades, pinning her to the bed. The way she transferred all the power to me and let me do whatever I wanted stirred the animal part of me. I wanted to consume her and care for her in one bite.

I stuck my fingers in her. "How often do you wake up wet?"

"Whenever you tell me to get on my knees."

I spread her knees, drawing my fingers along her seam. She groaned, and I pressed my other hand down on her.

"Open yourself for me."

She reached behind and pulled her thighs apart, pinkies separating the soft flesh of her ass cheeks.

I put my dick to her opening and slid inside her. I could have narrated how tight she was. How wet. What a perfect fit her cunt was. But I had other plans.

"Touch yourself. Make yourself come."

She twisted her arm between her legs and moved her finger over her clit. I felt her warming and tensing. I'd never met such a sexually responsive woman. I could fuck her forever. I could fuck her and say filthy things I could never say to anyone else. She was free. Unrepressed. An open door.

She started gasping, clenching and releasing, as I fucked her.

"Come. Show me how you come."

I pressed open her cheeks and watched her ass clench when she came as she was told.

"Fiona," I said, losing my own control, "I'm taking you back. I'm marking you where you're hurt. It's mine." My balls ached, and the pressure became too much.

I pulled out of her. One hand on her ass cheek, exposing her, and the other on my dick, I came where he'd hurt her. I didn't enter it, she wasn't ready for that, but I shot myself on her ass, coating it until it was salved with me.

When I was empty, I kissed her lower back and pressed my thumb to her asshole, entering it slowly and my juices letting it slide in.

"Oh, Elliot." She gasped in pleasure.

"This is mine," I said. "No one can hurt you again."

chapter thirty-eight.

FIONA

It wasn't until the late morning that I started to see his room in the sunlight. I noticed things he wouldn't have chosen. A picture frame with flowers. Curtains in a modern pattern. Too many Q-tips in the bathroom and, behind the towels, tampons. He'd had a girlfriend. She must be gone or on vacation. Who was she? Did he love her? Was I just a fling?

I couldn't believe I cared. I was literally seething with jealousy.

The feeling was new. It was a sticky, putrid ochre bubbling inside me, and it felt valid and important. It puffed out its diarrhea-yellow chest and pounded its ribcage and demanded to be heard because it was its own justification.

*He's mine.*

*He marked me.*

*There is no one else.*

He was in the small backyard, talking on the phone. Two cups in front of him. He'd made me tea. Did he make her tea?

Maybe if I'd had more experience with jealousy, I wouldn't have taken it so seriously. But I had no calluses, no scars, no pattern recognition. Just asking him what was happening with the woman who lived there wasn't even on the table.

I was about to go outside and spew at him when my phone rang. I woke from emotional suffocation.

The number was unknown. That usually meant a reporter or a random fan who got my forwarding information. I usually sent those to voice mail, but I needed to stall going outside in this mood.

"Hello?" I sounded impatient. I knew that.

Elliot sat outside, still on the phone, leaning back. Now that I knew the body under the clothes, I was rabidly aroused.

"Fi!"

"Jonathan?"

"I miss you in here." His vowels were thick and heavy.

"How did you get a phone?"

"You can get shit when you need it hey what's with Chilton he keeps saying something about paying him for something the same way you paid and I didn't know how much?"

There was no punctuation or pause in his sentence.

"You're drunk."

That alone was weird. Jonathan could pack it away without blinking an eye. If anything, whiskey made him sharper and more awake. I'd had to throw his keys in the pool twice because he swore he was alert enough to drive.

"I had a little I think I have a cold so it's worse."

"You let Warren get you whiskey? What the fuck is wrong with you? All you had to do was stay straight for a month."

"Pot kettle something something can you get me some money to pay him?"

"No. Jonathan. Stay away from him. Don't be alone with him. Do you understand? And he spiked that shit. Don't drink any more. Not a drop."

"Fuck you. You have no business—"

There was a scuffle on the other side. A rustle of clothes and some laughter.

Another voice came on. "Who is this?"

"Warren, you fuck."

"Fiona! Nice to—"

"You leave him alone, you hear me?" I turned away from Elliot and faced the corner. I couldn't get distracted. I couldn't take an ounce more input, or my panic and rage were going to set something on fire.

"Aw, why does it have to be like that?" said the little fucker.

"How much? How much do you want for the booze or whatever. Cash, okay?"

"Money' for the poor, Fiona. Come on. It's not that big a deal. You're okay, right? I hear you've been out with everyone a few times already."

The insinuation in his voice made me sick.

"Stay. Away. From. Him."

"He won't remember a thing."

"You fuck. I will murder you."

"Shoulda kept a dick in your mouth, sweetheart, instead of talking. See, I'm already incarcerated, and they're keeping me away from the girls now."

"Warren!"

But he wasn't there. It was just me and my shaking hands. My breath hitched in a sound that had no vowels.

"Your tea's cold." Elliot was at the door.

When I looked at him, my face must have betrayed the tangle of emotions. He came in and put his hands on my wrists, pulling them up so he could see my hands. When he saw the phone, he let them go.

"Who called?"

"My brother. You have to get Warren out."

"Out? Not after yesterday."

"*Now,*" I said.

"Why?"

"Warren spiked the shit he got Jonathan, and if not today, tomorrow he's going to pay the same way I did."

"I'll have the orderlies watch him."

"He's paying off half the orderlies!" I shouted. "The place is fucked."

Elliot breathed deeply and looked into my face, studying it for the truth behind the emotions. "And Jonathan's drunk?"

"Three sheets at eleven in the morning."

He put up a finger. "Good. Don't worry. I can get you through today."

"How?"

"Do you trust me?"

"I trust you to do what's right. But it might not be the right thing."

"It's the right thing."

"What are you going to do?"

He snapped his keys off the counter. "Abuse my power."

## chapter thirty-nine

FIONA

I sped north, shutting out everything but the route back to Malibu until my phone rang and my defenses crashed. I pulled off the exit and picked up the phone as I pulled into a gas station parking lot. It was Margie returning my call.

"Jonathan," I said. "You have to get Warren out or Jonathan or something."

I explained my call with our brother. I could hear her breathing when I was done, but she didn't speak for too long.

"What?" I asked. "Just say it."

"He's denying everything," she said. "He says it was—"

"Consensual. We knew he'd say that. That's why we got the rape kit."

More silence.

"What?"

"I just got out of the hearing. Westonwood fought it. They have a pack of lawyers. They make fifteen hundred an hour, these guys."

My heart sank. In the dead center of her silence were my worst fears. "Can we get Daddy's lawyers back?"

I heard a sniff from the other side. Jesus Christ, was she crying? Over this?

"Stop crying, Margie. This isn't over."

"It is. It's all over. The system is fucked. You can't win by doing things the right way in this world. No. There is no right and wrong. There's only what you get away with and what you don't."

"Okay, you know what? Thanks for the little pep talk. I'll be sure to slit my wrists after supper, but right now, Jonathan Drazen and Warren Chilton are trapped in a small box together, and one's a predator."

Another sniff. I waited. The morning fog blurred the horizon, and I counted cars going up PCH.

"I'll figure it out," she said.

"I will too. Don't forget to call."

"I love you," she said. "And I'm sorry."

My phone buzzed with another call. I looked at the screen. Elliot.

"I love you too."

I switched calls. "Elliot?"

"I have Jonathan in disciplinary isolation," he said softly.

"Is he safe?"

"I'm staying around to make sure. Chilton's in the rec room. Doesn't seem bothered."

"He's crazy."

"We have actual names for what he is. But crazy will do. Your brother can't get out of here any time soon. So the only way to separate them is to approve Warren's release next week. Is that what you want?"

Across from me was a hardware store parking lot with men sitting out front and waiting for a job, a convenience store, a garbage-strewn curb. None of it had anything to do with me. None of it had the answer. What did I want? I wanted to toss Warren to these men and tell them all what he did.

But I couldn't do that.

Warren would get out and go after Karen for fun. Then once Jonathan was released, he'd buddy up to him and make nice until my dumbass brother didn't know what hit him.

"Yes," I said. "That's what I want."

"There's a chance he'll be required to stay if the grand jury gets to it in time."

"They won't. Can you keep Jonathan in isolation for a whole week?"

"No. Forty-eight to seventy-two hours, max."

I slid down my seat. Huffed a breath.

"Where will you be later?" he asked.

I wanted him. His arms around me, his voice in my ear. With everything going on, his attention would soothe the memory of the police station. He could make it all go away for a few hours.

Just like a drug.

"Is it okay if I take some time?" I said. "I need a day to absorb everything. I feel overwhelmed."

He didn't answer right away.

"Of course it's fine."

We hung up. He'd paused before answering. Not too long, but long enough to make me wonder what it was about. Was he wondering whether or not to trust me? Did he want to mention that he expected me to be faithful, even when he wasn't around? Or was that just in my head?

I could obsess all day. Instead, I went home. I had to arrange getting Snowcone back to the stables, sell a car, take care of the practicalities of my life. Elliot could trust me. I just had to prove it.

chapter forty.

FIONA

I hadn't unpacked my things in Laurel Canyon in the first place. The biggest problem I had was finding where Deacon had put everything.

"What are you looking for?" Debbie asked.

"I don't know. I feel like I had more than this." I indicated the two small duffels on the bed.

"You didn't."

"How can that be?"

Debbie shrugged. "On Maundy, you wore what you were told, and when you wore something else, you got it from your own house."

The place with the walk-in closets so big they needed windows. The one with a room just for shoes. Right.

"About the other night," I said, and she stood up straighter. "Thank you. I know what you were trying to do. Give me back the control I gave up a long time ago."

She put her hands on my face and her nose to mine. She smelled of tea and citrus, and I had to resist the urge to kiss her.

"Did it work?" she asked.

"Yeah. Mostly. Maybe?" I shrugged and dug around for an honest answer. "I can't tell, actually. One night of topping you was great, but the jury's still out on life-changing."

She kissed me quickly then stepped back. I was grateful. It was hard to think with her standing so close.

"You were a child too long," she said.

"I don't know what I want to be when I grow up."

"Just be a grown-up."

Yeah. It wasn't that easy, but why should it be?

I grabbed one duffel and started for the other, but Debbie took it.

"You never answered me," I said. "About the connection between Deacon and me. If you saw it or not."

She handed me the bag. "With you and him, I couldn't figure it out. There's a linking, but it's not complete. Not one hundred percent. You'll always be connected to him. Maybe not in a way either of you likes or understands, but there is a small space you fill for each other."

"I feel like you fill a space too."

"With you and me, it's just human. You gave me something I needed. Thank you."

I dropped the bags and hugged her. She wrapped her arms around me.

"Will I see you again?" I asked.

"Yes. I promise. Yes."

I went to the door. I didn't think I was going to get out clean. Nothing could be easy, especially the hard things.

Deacon stood by my car, looking as though he was going to get in and drive it away without me. It was perfect for him. Proportioned for a man with broad shoulders and a crooked nose. He opened the trunk.

"You're letting me go?" I asked.

"You'll be back."

I almost said no. Never. Returning to him would be like taking a step backward, but what would be the point of saying that? To hurt him? He looked fine. He looked like nothing touched him, but it was an act. His shell was hard and as strong as stone, but I'd always known the way in.

I dropped my bags in the trunk and kissed his cheek, letting his smell of earth and leather fill me for the last time. He let me hold him, but he was guarded.

When I drove through the gate and saw him in the rearview, I knew I hadn't seen the last of him. Elliot called, but I didn't pick up. It would have been disrespectful to what had just happened. What I had just *done*.

I drove up the 405 to the 101 to the 110 to the 105 back up the 405...the Meditation Loop around Los Angeles.

I pulled off the freeway and into a spot when my phone rang. It was Elliot.

"Jonathan was almost out of isolation," he said.

"How? What the hell do you have to do in that place to get stuck in isolation?"

"Attack your therapist."

I put my head on the wheel and closed my eyes. "What if I just signed myself in?"

"I won't admit you. Not so you can do the job I should be doing."

"We don't have time to wait to see if you can do your job."

"I checked his room and Warren's room for more alcohol, and there isn't any."

"Bullshit. Did you check him for Rohypnol?"

"We would have found it."

I looked out the window but couldn't see a thing past the glass. It was all colors and edges, movement and stillness. Nothing meant anything.

"He knows," I said. "And if you pay too much attention to him, you're going to expose yourself. You'll be a disgraced therapist."

I used Deacon's words because they were right. He was going to lose his work and feel more shame than he could bear, both for his affair with me and for manipulating Westonwood's system. That would be my fault. I'd dragged him into this, and he'd already done too much, told me too much, broken who-even-knew-how-many codes and ethics.

"Do you like your work?" I asked.

"Yes, I do. But I like you better."

"Do you believe in responsibility? Like, to heaven. Not the law or the rules. But that God or whatever knows what's your fault and what you should have done to make it right, and if you don't, you've done wrong? Even if something wasn't directly your fault, but you caused it with some stupid decisions and you let bad shit happen when you could have stopped it? That kind of responsibility."

"I think that's a hamster on a wheel."

"I want to start over. I want a clean slate. I can't bear it. Everything that makes me happy hurts someone."

There was a long silence. A truck went by so fast my car lifted a little on its struts and dropped, as if it wanted to get ripped into the draft but was too heavy.

"It's not your fault, Fiona."

"Not yet it's not."

I heard a beep on his side.

"I have to go. When am I seeing you tonight?"

"I'll call you," I said.

## chapter forty-one

FIONA

Crazy Fiona. I'd always been Crazy Fiona. It was easy. I just did what I wanted when I wanted. I loved my life, even the parts I hated. I saw myself through other people's eyes and knew only their need to be entertained.

I'd had a job to do, and I did it.

I still wanted flake. I still wanted sex. I still wanted to live in a lens.

But I didn't want to want to.

I wanted to feel the all-over everything of a really clean high and the freedom of a new dick, but I had a voice in my head telling me to just go one more day without them. I'd done good work. Don't throw it all away.

And the other voice in my head said, "It's for a good cause. You can do what you want one more time. Just one more time… to save Jonathan."

Fucking voice.

***

I didn't know how to walk that razor, and once the flake started flowing, I had no way to keep my balance. It would go however it would go.

Elliot came to my place after his day at Alondra. I peeled off his clothes, and he watched as I removed mine. Every time we fucked, he got a little bossier, a little more dominating, a little rougher. He'd never be Deacon. But if I wanted Deacon, I'd be with him.

The sun had set completely when he wrapped himself around me.

"I need to get back in," I said. "Before Warren figures out a way to get to Jonathan."

"We're watching him. Don't you trust me?"

"I trust you, but I don't trust the world. Can you take me in? Commit me? Just say the therapy is going bad?"

"You'd have to be a danger to yourself or others."

"Tell them I'm a danger to myself."

"But you're not. You're a danger to me."

I rolled on top of him. "I admire your faith. I admire how you want to do things the right way."

"You say it like you can't do the same."

It hadn't occurred to me that I was incapable, only that I was outside those rules. For better or worse, what had bound other people had never bound me.

"I know you won't save me from myself," I said. "If I'm doing something stupid, I have to just do it and face the consequences. But this is different. This is my brother, and you know as well as I do that he's in no position to deal with this himself. And I've got nothing on Warren. No proof he intends to do anything, and what are you going to do with a psycho's fucking intentions anyway? So we can muck around with the authorities all we want, and what happened to me is going to happen to my brother. I won't have that on my head. He was brought up the same way I was, and I know what it's like. He needs time to grow up, and Warren's going to take it away from him."

He kissed me. "I admire your nobility and your loyalty. It's beautiful. It makes me crazy about you. But it makes me afraid for you too. If you go back in, you're separated from me. I don't want that ever again. I want us going forward, not back."

I kissed him. He bit my bottom lip, gently keeping me from moving away.

He was right. My thinking was too literal and limited. Maybe there was another way to do this.

# chaprty forty-two.

FIONA

I'd done the unthinkable. I'd spoken to outsiders about what happened between the privileged. We were the mafia. We were the law. We did not break the silence about what we did to each other.

"Is Baby here?" I asked Jack.

His chin was scratched raw under his lip and his hair had a bald patch. He kept playing with the area around it. "I don't know where she's at."

"What about Karen?"

"Nah, man."

"What's wrong with you?" I slapped his hand away from the bald patch by his ear. A hair was trapped between two fingers.

"They won't even talk to you if you find them."

We were on a Hollywood rooftop with a pool and pod chairs, twelve stories up. The roof was surrounded by three-foot-high stone walls that made you feel like you were about to fall onto Sunset.

I wore a bikini like all the other girls. Below us, the lights of a movie premier cast shafts into the sky. The music was low, the paparazzi waited in a pack on the sidewalk, and limos lined up around the block.

"Jackey!" Baby came between us, putting her arms around Jack. Her pink bag was open like a mouth spitting hundreds. Her chin was striped with pink scratch marks. "Do you have any more tar?"

"A little."

"Hey," I said, "I was looking for you."

She ignored me and whispered in Jack's ear. He swallowed. She moved her hand between his legs, and his eyes fluttered closed. Derek pulled me to the dance floor before I had to witness whatever it was Baby would have been happy for me to witness.

I turned. "Don't leave before I talk to you," I said to Baby.

She didn't even look at me when she held up her middle finger.

I called Karen while I gyrated against Derek. No answer.

Derek pulled up my bikini top while we danced, running his thumbs across my nipples. I pulled it back down. Derek's hands on me snapped me into a clarity where Elliot saw me with another man. I felt what he would have felt. I thought what he would have thought. The pain was palpable.

I wasn't there to hurt Elliot. I was there to talk to Baby. I needed to feel her out, see if she thought Daddy Chilton would cut a deal before his son turned into a PR nightmare.

"Have you seen Karen?" I asked Derek.

He put his arms around me and swayed his hips. "Nope." He untied the back of my bikini top.

"Jesus." I pulled away, feeling for the strings. "Quit it." I tied the top back together.

"Is this what it is now?" he asked in my ear. "You're a prude *and* a rat?"

Funny how not doing a bunch of drugs or fucking anyone who asked was considered weird. Or how telling the cops you were raped made you an outsider. But who could blame him? We had procedures in our world, and I wasn't following them.

"I'm both and more, asshole." I noticed a little mark on his chin, and I poked it. "What's this? Is this Jack's shit?"

"You should try it. Might make you normal again."

I nodded. It was probably fantastic. A high like no other. I turned and faced the pool, dropping my phone onto my little red chamois. Derek grabbed me from behind and I kicked him back. My foot landed near my phone and skidded, knocking it into the pool.

Crap.

The phone went vertical and accelerated to the bottom, landing soundlessly. I dove in. The water was bath warm, and the underwater lights made the black, and now useless, device easy to find. I scooped it up and swam for the surface.

When my head popped up from the surface and I felt the cold air on my face, saw the stars above, heard the sounds of the fans and people downstairs, I felt a gratitude and happiness for my simple existence on the earth. It was like being high, but not like that at all.

"Did you hear about Karen?" someone said next to me.

I snapped out of my reverie. It was Arrow.

"Hear what?" I asked, flipping my phone open. Yeah. Useless.

"Her parents found coke in her sheets and committed her."

"She's in Westonwood?" I waded to the edge and tossed my phone onto the tiles.

"Guess so."

"Huh." I lifted myself out of the water and pivoted until I was sitting on the edge. Karen was inside. She needed it, and I was glad she was getting help, but I wished it was anywhere but Westonwood.

"Hey, Fee," Arrow said from the pool. "You look good."

"Really?"

He'd taken me by surprise, sincerity all over his face.

"Yeah. Kind of, you know. Together." He nodded, eyes narrowed as if seeing something for the first time. "Kinda cool."

"Thanks, Arrow. You're all right."

He winked at me and leaned back into the water, swimming away from my all-rightness.

I got out of the pool and snapped up my chamois, leaving a path of water drops and wet footprints through the bar.

The locker rooms were paneled in dark teak and floored in warm matte marble. Orchids marked the empty spaces between the sinks, and the lockers weren't even locked for the private party. I flipped mine open.

I had to tell Elliot that Warren was after Karen, but my phone was useless. I tapped the back, pushed the green button, shook it for whatever that was worth. The black screen just mocked me.

I heard a laugh I recognized from one of the shower stalls. Outside it, on the floor, sat a pink Prada bag.

"Baby!" I said. "Can I use your phone?"

*I need to tell my therapist your brother is going to rape Karen as payment for amphetamines.*

The shower door popped open. Baby was naked, back to the wall, finger between her legs. Her other hand scratched her lower lip. Jack stood against the opposite wall, watching her.

"If you can find it in my bag," she said, and under her breath, she added, "bitch."

Jack snapped the bag away and held it out of my reach.

"Jack," I said, holding out my hand, "a minute. It won't take a minute."

"You called me a nerd when we were in the nuthouse. Who's the nerd now?"

"You're still a nerd, Jack. Own it. Now give me the bag."

"If I'm a nerd, what are you?"

"I'm a prude and a rat." I reached for the bag, but he snapped it away. Baby still danced in a shower stall with her fingers between her legs.

"Kiss Baby, and I'll give you the phone."

"No."

"No?" Baby asked. She acted as if I'd just stuffed Santa back up the chimney.

"I'm just not in the mood."

I could have explained there was someone in my life I didn't want to hurt. That kissing another human being would jeopardize a relationship that already wasn't supposed to exist. But I didn't have the energy, and I wanted the phone.

"Never mind," I said. There were a hundred phones on the other side of the door. "Baby, when you're done here, I just want to talk."

"About?"

"Your brother."

She shot out a little laugh through the thick soup of her high. "You talked enough."

I shot a look at Jack, who had put the bag down and was rubbing black stringy tar out of a little glass jar.

"He's going to be embarrassing. I can take it all back. Say I lied. But I need a meeting with your dad."

She smiled. "You Drazens all have daddy issues."

"Open," Jack said. She opened her mouth, and he tucked a bit of tar between her gum and lower lip.

Baby continued, "Every time Warren fucks someone else, it's one less time he fucks me."

I absorbed what she said but didn't have time to react before I was fed the image of Jack putting his tar-coated finger between her legs. She gasped. Groaned. Her eyes went wide, and she cried out then came with a shriek.

"Holy *shit*!" she said then thrust her hips forward and came again.

"I tell you what," Jack said to me. "For the purpose of scientific inquiry, I didn't see you take a drink yet. I want to see how this stuff works on clean blood." He scraped the jar of the last of it. "You give this a shot, and I'll make sure my uncle gets you a meeting with Daddy Chilton. He's in town until Tuesday morning, I think. Then he's filming in like Zululand or something."

Baby was still in the throes of ecstasy.

"Was that safe? To put it on her clit like that?"

"No clue. It works on membranes. I'm experimenting with adding a little K before I go wide. Come on."

Jack actually could get the meeting through his uncle, who was a studio head and a big player in the Hollywood old boys' network. And he could get it soon.

"You better come through, or you're going to be the sorriest nerd in California," I said.

Baby groaned and slid down the wall.

"Open up."

"You're putting it where everyone else does," I said. "Lip only."

I opened my mouth. He wedged his finger in the front and slid it across.

"I always liked you, Fiona." He took his finger out.

"I never disliked you, Jack. But I'm starting to."

I had more to say, but my thoughts were drowned out by two things: Baby screaming "Make it stop, make it stop," then clenching, thrusting, pushing against the wall, and my brain flooding with an explosion of endorphins. I had the most unmotivated sense of well-being and bliss I'd ever experienced. This was more than an orgasm. More than emotional happiness. More than a feeling of safety and joy. It wasn't like coke, where I felt *like* God, or LSD, where I thought I *saw* God.

I became one with God in a blinding eruption of love.

I couldn't even feel my body.

I was trying too hard to get out of my skin to engage a sound or feeling. It was like blacking out without the blackness. Losing consciousness without sleeping. Being engulfed in a light so bright it wasn't visible.

A quiet voice in the light said, "Never, ever do this again."

At the end of that thought, I became aware of my face at the top of my chin, where the gum curved into lip. It itched a little, then like mad, growing into a fury of tingling deep inside the muscle.

When I scratched it, I tipped, and something in me said I shouldn't fall over, whatever I did. I became aware of weight on one elbow, and realized I was on my hands and knees. Lifting a hand to scratch had thrown off my balance.

I got up on my knees and clawed my chin.

"Fiona! Get down!"

The voice sounded like a stereo turned down then up then down really fast.

A blue light cut through the black light.

Then a red light.

And a blue light.

And the sound of a *whop whop whopping* helicopter.

Deacon, who shouldn't have been anywhere near that rooftop, had a voice that reminded me of feeling safe and right when I felt most vulnerable. I opened my eyes. Or maybe they were already open and I decided to use them to see.

On my right, just below me, Deacon raised his arms. "Get down. Just get down."

On my left, a twelve-story drop onto Sunset Boulevard.

"Baby," I said. "Is she okay?"

"She's fine."

The music had stopped. An ambulance was parked outside, flashing its lights, and the paparazzi were huddled across the street with their black Cyclops eyes looking at me.

"You're lying," I said. The itch in my chin was furious.

"Come down, and we can talk about it."

"I'm scared."

"You don't have to be," he said.

"I can't stand up."

"Fall. I'll catch you."

I tipped a little to the right, then more, and fell into white sheets on a thin mattress with a white light humming over me.

## chapter forty-three

FIONA

My gums felt as if they were on fire, and my spine hurt between my shoulder blades, all the way up to my neck. I felt as though someone was pinching the top of my hand, but when I opened my eyes, I saw the IV bag hanging over me, and I knew where I was.

I took a deep breath.

Something rustled. To the right and at the foot of the bed. My senses were back, and I smelled him there. I hadn't placed his scent before.

"Has anyone ever told you that you smell like the air before it rains?" I said.

He didn't answer.

"I'm sorry," I continued.

"Me too."

"I can explain."

I moved my hand. It wasn't tied down. I touched my chin and pressed at the cleft where it met my lower lip, relieving the itch in my gums.

"I'm sure you can."

I hitched myself up on my elbows. I was in Westonwood blues. He was in a tan suit and blue tie, his elbows on his knees and his arms draped between them as if fully engaged in something he didn't understand. Loving me.

I felt like a clown.

"What were you thinking?" Elliot asked.

"That I was taking a cab home."

He smiled and looked at the floor.

"I didn't go with Deacon," I said. "He showed up there."

"I know."

"How do you know?"

"He told me he didn't bring you, and he's a lot of things, but he's not a liar. And also, I followed you."

"Elliot!"

He put his finger to his lips to remind me that no one should hear. "That makes me an asshole. Fine. But I thought you might pull a stunt to get back in here. And here you are. Well done."

I flopped back down. "I had a completely different stunt planned."

I put my forearm over my eyes to cut the light. I saw the night in a flash. The pool. The roof. The locker room.

"Baby," I said.

"Yeah?"

"No." I moved my arm away and stared into the light. "Baby Chilton. Is she all right?"

"I guess. You were the only casualty. You're all over the news."

"I don't give a shit about that."

I didn't. Baby was all right, at least physically. That mattered to me. I'd had nothing to do with her episode in the shower, but I felt responsible somehow. I was sure Jack had put the tar on her pussy to show off to me what it could do.

Elliot stood over me, blocking the light. I wished he'd put his hands on me, but he had a sort of detachment about him, and I felt ashamed of what I'd done. Again.

"So what's the deal? Am I fifty-one-fiftied again?"

"You checked yourself in."

"I did?"

"The paramedics gave you a choice: the ER or a mental facility. And here you are. Outpatient probation broken." He put his hands on either side of me and leaned in, blocking out the light, the room, everything. "Now, how am I going to keep you away from Warren Chilton?"

"You're not."

"I'm passing you to another therapist."

"Obviously. Since you're fucking me."

"I want you to leave Warren alone. Give him enough rope to hang himself."

"Am I a disappointment?" I asked.

"I knew what I was getting into with you."

I put my palm on his cheek. He hadn't shaved, and the roughness under my hand was pleasantly tactile. "I asked if you were disappointed."

"I'm not going to lie. I should say 'thank you' and walk away right now. I'm surprised at myself. I'm a sensible guy. I think things through, and anything that's too risky—I don't do. But you woke something up in me. I was dead. My life was dead. Then you came, and I feel God in you. I hear him in your voice. The crazy shit you do…he speaks to me. I don't know how long I'll last on a roller coaster. But all I want right now is for you to get out of here so I can experiment with your body."

"Will God keep talking to you if I stop doing crazy shit?"

"I hope I find out soon."

I didn't want to promise him anything. Promises were for children and people who weren't worthy of trust. So I didn't say a word to him, but I spoke to myself.

I promised myself he'd find out what it was like to be with sane Fiona. Not normal Fiona. Not staid, conservative Fiona. Not a Fiona who made all the least risky choices and didn't break any rules. That Fiona didn't exist, and trying to create her wouldn't do shit but make me miserable.

But he could get to know sober Fiona. Straight Fiona. Faithful Fiona. I could work hard, stay monogamous, and still be the force of nature he saw God in.

In his ocean-colored eyes, I saw my own potential. With a little work, I could become those things for him and, more importantly, for myself.

chapter forty-four.

ELLIOT

Obviously, I had no interest in emotional self-preservation. I couldn't even bring myself to consider leaving her.

I was crazier than she was.

I'd seen this type of thing go bad, read the case studies, talked a few dozen couples through nightmares of drugs, alcohol, and unpredictable behavior. I didn't understand why anyone would put themselves through what those people put themselves through, but I counseled them anyway. I'd been the perfect example of ignorance. I didn't know what made them love each other because I didn't understand love.

And that was why I didn't feel threatened by the fact that Deacon Bruce was in my Westonwood office. He loved her. I got it. I had as much compassion for him as I had for myself.

"Mister Bruce," I said, closing the door behind me.

He was sitting in the leather chair by the window as if it was his office, not mine. He wore a dark suit and white shirt open two buttons, revealing a leather string tied around his neck. A bone-colored pendant in the shape of a cornucopia dangled from it. "You need to let her go."

"I can't." I started for my desk but stopped. I didn't want to sit behind a barrier. I put my files down and sat across from him. The light from the window behind him kept his face in darkness and must have exposed my every expression.

"You're the one managing her probation."

"Not anymore."

He didn't make a move. He was pure control, and I wondered for the first time why he needed to regulate Fiona. I saw his cracks and knew his secrets in that moment. His life was out of control, and without her, it spun away.

"You found her in a weakened state, and you took advantage of your position." He spoke as if broadcasting the news. All facts. "She came here, confused and willing to hear whatever anyone said. She idealized you, then you found a way in. You used tricks like hypnosis. You manipulated her vulnerability. For what? What's your game? Are you her therapist or her lover? Because you know as well as I do that you can't be both."

And in those few words, I was on the defensive.

"You need to let her go," I said, turning the subject away from the lines I'd crossed.

"You don't have the tools to give her what she needs. You're weak. If you loved her, you'd take care of her. You'd do what she needed you to do." His voice was absent jealousy or venom. He spoke as if we were two men with a common interest, and his was superior.

"It doesn't work like that. She needs to make her own life."

"You're going to let Warren Chilton rape her again?"

The "again" was loaded. It implied I'd let it happen the first time. I tamped down my desire to defend myself. I didn't have to. I hadn't done anything wrong. I hadn't failed, even if I felt as though I had.

"You thought I didn't know who did it or where it happened," he said. "She told me last night, before the ambulance came for her. She was raped under your care, and now I'm supposed to roll over and let you have her? You underestimate me."

"What do you think I should do? Arrange her release? What caseworker in their right mind would put her back in a police cruiser to go home after she was found on a twelve-story ledge, fucked up on a designer drug? Or I should find a way to get Chilton out so he can continue his psychotic spree in society?"

"She is your priority. Not society."

"It's all my responsibility. All of it. I don't get to pick and choose."

He sprang up and stood over me. "That's the problem."

I wouldn't be cowed. I wouldn't be intimidated. Not every decision I'd made had been perfect, but I'd be damned if I would be told I didn't love her the right way.

I stood. He was two inches taller, and I was over six feet.

"The problem, Mister Bruce, is that you've done nothing but baby her. You've continued the damage her parents did. Your boundaries are constructs. They don't give her the power to make the right decision. You don't let her fail because you design failures that are irrelevant and you train her behavior to mold into your world, not the real world. You fucked this up. You fucked it all up. You took a woman who could have figured her life out, and you turned her into a pet who couldn't wait to run away as soon as you left the gate open."

I thought he recognized the truth in what I was saying. Or maybe I needed to believe that. But he seemed to soften just a little, enough for me to continue.

"You need to let her be," I said.

"So you can take her?"

And there, in its full and splendid glory, was the reason therapists shouldn't fall in love with their patients. It muddied the waters to thick paste. I lost my ability to advise both Fiona and her enabler. Neither could trust me.

"You know what's right. Just do it." I opened the door. "Let me figure out what to do with Warren."

He stepped toward the doorway but stopped long enough to say, "I'll figure out what to do with him. Here's what you do. You understand that she's mine. You understand that what you did was wrong, and you go back to your God and ask for forgiveness. You do not stand in the way of what she needs, now or ever, because I will expose you. I won't have to lay a finger on you to destroy you."

And with that, he strode off as if taking care of Chilton was his responsibility.

What a fucking mess.

Frances made her way down the hall, passing him. She gave him the once-over, head to toe, then nodded, smiling, and turned her head as he walked by.

"Chapman," she said before I could close the door, "I want to talk to you."

She slipped in, and I shut the door behind her.

"Who was that?" she asked, sinking into the seat Deacon had just vacated.

"You want his number?"

"Jealous? You're cute too. I'm just used to you."

"He wants Fiona Drazen released to his care."

"And? Do you have a recommendation?"

"A few days observation."

She held up her file. "By someone else, apparently."

"I wasn't able to help her before—"

"So you're abdicating? That's not like you. As a matter of fact—"

"I haven't gotten anywhere," I said.

"Are we still talking about her therapy?"

"What does that mean?"

"I've been doing this a long time. I've seen nearly a thousand kids come in and out of this facility, and I've managed dozens of doctors. I've seen how they stand with each other. How they talk. I've seen you and the Drazen girl in the same room, and what I see is that you're too damned handsome for your own good—"

"Frances, really?"

"Tell me what's going on."

"No."

"We could get in a lot of trouble," she said.

"You won't."

"Besides the core ethical ickiness."

I crossed my legs. "Are you making an accusation?"

"I'm prying directly into the place where your business intersects with mine."

"There is no such place."

"I sense you're deflecting." She crossed her legs to match mine and upped the ante by crossing her wrists over her knee.

"You must have been amazing in session."

"I was. And you're still deflecting."

"I came to you with a serious problem," I said. "Fiona was raped by Warren Chilton on the grounds of this facility. What did you do? You took me off his case, and he's still walking around like he owns the joint. Let's address that core ethical ickiness."

"He denied it."

"Welcome back to the nineteen-fifties."

"Please"—she waved as if there was nothing there—"give me a break."

"Tell me what Rob Chilton's people said about Warren's habits. And I mean habits. Fiona's not the first or last. You know it. They know it. Is the Chilton Foundation putting a new wing on the place? Paying double?"

"Enough." She straightened her legs and leaned forward. "The matter is under investigation." She stood. "Until the authorities come back with something to nail him, like actual evidence, there's nothing I can do."

I stood and walked toward the door. "This has been such a fun little chat. Was there something you wanted?"

"I enjoy the hell out of you, Chapman. I'd hate to see your career end over a little ickiness."

It was doomed to end over something. Old age. Exhaustion. Death. Might as well be love.

chapter forty-five.

FIONA

"This is like déjà vu all over again," I said.

Frances smiled with an undertone of superiority then slid the papers across the table.

"I bet this happens all the time, actually."

"Everyone's different," she said noncommittally. "Some people need to do this a couple of times. Sometimes we have to switch methods. Try new things."

I scribbled my name on familiar forms. "Such as?" I was just making conversation.

"We're putting you in a group session," she said.

"Okay."

Whatever. I could do a group. Not a big deal. I didn't feel as if I needed to have Elliot in a room to myself. He and I could wait. We were solid.

"We'll do everything possible to keep you away from Warren Chilton."

My blood froze, and I stopped signing.

"But you have to meet us halfway," she said. "Stay where you belong. We closed off the holes in the fence back there, but you guys are smart. I'm sure there are more little hideouts. Stay away from them. I've scheduled you for different mealtimes, but you're to steer clear of each other in the halls and everywhere else."

"You're making it my responsibility to stay away from my rapist?"

"I'm asking you to participate in preventing it from happening again. You asked to be here. I'd be happy to transfer you to a different facility."

I had no recollection of asking to be at Westonwood. It must have seemed like the best option at the time, or the best way to get to Warren. My stoned self was far braver than my sober self. Time would tell if she was any smarter.

The option to switch out did have its appeal. Starting clean and participating, as she said, could be very productive, yet it felt like running away. I had business to attend to here.

"Is Jonathan still here? I don't have to avoid him, do I?" I tried to sound non-threatening, but I'd somehow poked her, because she smiled again.

"No. He's been asking for you."

I dotted the last i on the last form and pushed it back to her. "Great. Thank you."

"The MD is going to look at you in an hour so we can review your medications."

"I'll be ready," I said.

I left the office fully-charged, the exact opposite of angry. I didn't forget Warren for a second, nor did I forget what my brother needed from me, but I felt as if I was in Westonwood for my own good, and I could make something of it.

chapter forty-six.

FIONA

Westonwood hadn't changed. I had. Through the lens of my time outside, most of which was spent without drugs or sex, Westonwood seemed more hopeful a place, sunnier, brighter. I walked the halls looking for Jonathan and talked to a few people I'd seen before, but I didn't get a sense of where he could be during the free hour.

It wasn't until the lunch break was nearly over, and I was sitting on a bench by the basketball courts, that I saw him loping toward an errant ball. He saw me, scooped up the ball, and dribbled toward me. Had he gotten taller? He looked as if he'd crested six feet in his weeks at Westonwood, and though he was as graceful as ever, he treated his limbs like new attachments. I swelled with protective warmth.

"I knew you'd be back," he said, throwing himself into the seat next to me as if he were indestructible.

"Nice, you had such faith in me."

"You didn't look ready when you left." He spun the ball on his finger, whipping it around until the black lines blurred.

"How was your hangover the other day?"

He popped the ball up and caught it. "How did you know?"

"You called me. Presumably on Warren's phone?"

He neither confirmed nor denied any of it. He flicked the surface of the ball, making an echoey pinging sound. "What did I say?"

"You asked for money."

He shook his head and spun the ball on his finger again. My brother was brilliant but an avoider of things that made him uncomfortable. Eventually, he'd probably avoid me altogether. Might as well get on with it.

"You know who I saw last week?" I asked. "Mindy and Baby."

He kept spinning the ball. No reaction.

"They asked about you."

"Say hi for me if you get out."

"Jon?"

"Yeah." He didn't stop with the ball.

I wanted to shove it down his throat. Instead I just clapped it between my palms and held it. "They had a lot to say about you."

He looked at me for the first time. "What's that mean?"

"I don't know what your relationship with Rachel was, or if it involved you fucking other people. Or if you're a cheat or what. I don't know. But nothing you do is private."

"I'm not a cheat."

"Good. Hold on to that. I heard them talking about stuff I didn't even want to envision."

He shrugged. It wasn't a denial that he'd fucked half of Hollywood, but it wasn't an admission. That was fine with me.

"It's not easy being whatever it is we are," I said. "And we hang out in our own circles so we don't have to explain ourselves. Like why we never fly commercial or why we don't… whatever…cook a meal because why should we? But look at Margie. She's almost normal. I think she's got it right. She's, like, in the world, you know?"

"Yeah, well, old money fucks old money. Sometimes it fucks new money. There's a reason for that shit."

Rachel hadn't had much in the way of money, and in his adolescent mind, staying away from the likes of her equaled staying away from middle-class girls.

"Warren fucks Baby. How about that for a reason to stay away from them?"

He twisted his face until he looked as if he was wearing a blender.

"I know," I said. "It's fucking gross. She told me as much. I have no idea how consensual it is, but she flipped it off. And they have a younger brother, so I don't even want to know."

"I'm going to be sick."

"You did fuck her, didn't you?"

He put the ball on his knees and put his forehead to it. "I thought we had problems."

"We do. But I think you should avoid him. I don't want that brand of crazy rubbing off."

"I can't believe you'd even suggest that shit."

"He's fucking crazy. No more booze. Don't take anything from him. When you called me…I know rohypnol when I hear it."

"Man"—he leaned back—"I don't even remember any of that. Woke up in a padded room."

"Did anything hurt?"

He looked at me with those emerald-green eyes, the sounds of inmates playing basketball behind him. I should have paused before asking or maybe couched the question.

"Such as?" he asked.

"Anything unexpected."

"My arms from trying to get out of the straps."

We stared at each other for a second. Then two.

"Why?" he asked softly.

"Because Warren made that call, I was able to get someone here to put you in solitary. You're welcome. Stay away from him."

"What did he do to you?"

He'd find out soon enough when he got out and the news was the news. But all was silent in Westonwood, and I had to continue to protect Jonathan the same way I protected Deacon. But I couldn't say nothing.

The bell rang. It was time to get to our business.

"It doesn't matter." I stood. "He's not an appropriate friend. That's all."

"Thanks, Mom."

I snapped the ball away. "I'll leave that to Margie."

I threw it at a hoop, missed by a mile, and took off for the main building.

## chapter forty-seven

ELLIOT

I watched her talk to her brother on the side of the basketball courts and felt the connection between us. The rope had heft and drag, as if it was as real as the nose on my face. I was done denying it.

So what to do about my work?

Frances had been very clear about her suspicions. Her conversation had almost been a warning salvo that I had to make choices, and they'd have consequences.

How long could I tread water and do both at the same time? The rules were clear. A therapist could see a patient two years after the therapy ended. I had no chance of waiting that long. And with Fiona's public persona, I had even less chance of keeping it a secret for two years.

The bell rang. My session would be here in seconds. A young woman with profound feelings of isolation was going to sit across from me, and she needed my full attention. On the basketball court, Fiona took a shot at the hoop and missed before she trotted into the building I watched from.

"I'm sorry I'm asking for something again," I said softly to no one and the only one who mattered. "I love my work. I don't want to lose it. I'm not trying to be transactional. I need some help figuring this out."

No answer. At least not in the form of the clouds parting and a bearded guy telling me to get my shit together, deal with the consequences, and trust him.

"I trust you," I said, and I meant it.

I took a breath and let the worry go so I could do the job I loved.

chapter forty-eight.

FIONA

I put my Westonwood blues back on. The doctor had run through his examination quickly, focusing on the blood work and sparing me another pelvic. He was bald but for a few strands on top of his head, and his hands were bulbous and creased. He asked for a rundown of what he'd find, and I gave him the list without apology. I wasn't defiant or brazen. I wasn't contrite either. I didn't owe him an apology. I owed him a list of the drugs I'd taken in the past week. When I told him what I remembered of Jack's description of the tar, he looked at me over the top of his glasses.

"Ricin?"

I shrugged. "It was loud. It was *ricinus something*. He might as well have been speaking another language."

"He was." The doc made a note and left the nurse to finish.

She took blood, my temperature, checked my reflexes. The arm band squeezed so tight to get my pressure, I thought blood would never circulate through to my fingers again. The doctor had come back to listen to my heartbeat and left me to get dressed.

I thought I'd gotten through to Jonathan. Nothing like grossing someone out to make a point. I'd have to remember that. Of course, Warren still had one over on my brother, and he would try to make my brother pay for it.

I didn't know what to do about that.

The nurse directed me to the doc's office. It was richly painted in greens and cranberries, like a year-round Christmas theme. I threw myself into the upholstered chair, leaving the wooden one in front of his desk empty.

"All right, well…" He cleared his throat. "Most of this will take some time to get back, but we did a quick run on a couple of things. You've been sexually active?"

"Yes." *Duh.*

He looked at me over his glasses. "You're pregnant."

He could have shocked me more. Like if he'd said I was growing a furry tail or a penis. Or if he'd said I was actually the love child of Whoopi Goldberg and Bruce Lee.

"I have an IUD. Those are, like, one hundred percent effective."

"No," he said. "You don't."

"What?"

He held up a piece of typed paper with a signature on the bottom. My signature. "We checked you when you came in the first time. Weeks ago. The IUD had passed its expiry date, and we removed it."

"What? How did I not feel that?"

"You were medicated. It doesn't hurt to remove anyway."

"Was I stoned when I signed this?" I snapped the paper away from him.

"No. You signed the next day."

I'd signed off on understanding this the first time I was released, an hour before I got into Deacon's car. Well, crap. Crap crap crap. I'd always been careful. I'd never had to have an emergency D&C. Never took a morning-after pill. Never missed a period.

"Wait. Doesn't it take weeks for the tests to know?"

"Blood tests can detect pregnancy days after conception."

What the hell was I supposed to do?

And what had I done to my body in the past week?

"Is it okay?" I asked. "I smoked. And there was that thing I took last night—"

"Two nights ago."

"I don't even know what it was. Did I hurt it?"

And did it matter?

And whose was it?

"We won't know until you get a CVS at twelve weeks. The meds you're on aren't contraindicated, but I'm lowering your dose."

Jesus Christ. I didn't know who the father was.

Another item on the list of things that may or may not matter.

"Would you like to discuss your options?" the doctor asked.

How long had I been staring at that paper?

"No," I said. "Not right now." I didn't think I could discuss options until I'd absorbed what had happened.

"All right. If you want to use the phone to tell your family, I'm sure it's allowed."

I walked down the hall, crossing the cafeteria. I saw Warren sitting next to the ping-pong table before I saw Jonathan hitting the ball back over the net to someone I didn't know. Warren made eye contact with me, his expression flat and charmless as if he never felt a thing about anything. Then he smiled, and I realized I'd seen his true self in that unguarded second. Just emotional emptiness he had to fill every single minute of every single day.

Jonathan's back was to me. He dropped his paddle and shook his opponent's hand. Warren and I were still bound by our stare, his vacant smile, the breakneck swirl of guilt and shame over a bean of a baby. I wondered if he could see inside me, but I knew he couldn't. I was having feelings, hot and cold, up and down, a broken narrative of thoughts spitting out waves of anger, joy, confusion, helplessness. He'd never had an emotion. Not about anything. He couldn't see mine. He craved my feelings, fed on them, was so curious about them he'd rape me to create them.

I hadn't chosen what to do about the baby, but when I walked away from the cafeteria, it wasn't because I was afraid for myself. I had another person to protect.

## chapter forty-nine

FIONA

I skipped dinner. Skipped rec time. Skipped talking. Skipped thinking. Went to group session in the afternoon because it would be noticed if I didn't, and my feet hurt from standing by the window.

I couldn't get a space on one of the Herman Miller chairs, so I sat next to another girl who had her hands in her lap. She bounced her knees as if they were fully gassed-up pistons. I didn't want to talk to her or the four people across from us. They had ennui, depression, a case of the existential blues. Too much tickle and not enough slap.

And guiding us through all of this was Brazilian blowout. Dr. Deanna.

"Yesterday, we talked about Quentin's last night out before he came here, and his feelings of—"

Good times.

Could I eat the organic, locally grown, handmade crackers? Was starch bad? Was there too much salt? Was I even keeping this thing? Never mind who the father was, how was I quali-fied to be a mother?

"We've had some very productive discussions, so—"

Did I have to tell the father? Would I tell both of them? Neither? Would I just get rid of it and smile happily at Elliot and pretend I didn't have cause to see Deacon ever again?

"But first, I wanted to make sure we all know—"

And then what?

And why?

"Would you like to introduce yourself to—"

Did I have something better to do?

Was I broke? Orphaned? Sick?

Did I have nothing at all to offer a baby?

"I have something to offer," I said to myself but loudly enough that Deanna thought I was speaking to her.

"Go on," she said.

Six sets of over-privileged eyes stared at me in varying shades of curiosity and distrust. I hadn't wanted to speak. I was just going to say hello and go back to my room to brood. But they expected something from me now, and it wasn't to feed their egos or entertain them but to help them.

"I…"

Swallow.

"I have a lot to offer. I'm a good friend. A good sister. I protect people who are important to me. I can teach someone about the world, about what to expect. I can help them avoid my mistakes. I'm honest with people even if it hurts me. And I'm funny sometimes. And brave." I sat straighter, because I felt the truth in that one. From bone to skin, I knew it was true, so I repeated it.

"I am brave."

FIONA

I slept. I didn't know if it was the meds or the after-effects of Jack's stupid tar shit. But I left session without elaborating or speaking again, and I went to my room and slept.

When I woke, I knew something for sure.

I had to tell Elliot and Deacon.

I was keeping the baby, and I had to tell them. If I was brave, and I was, then that was what had to be done. Toying with any other options was cowardly shit, and I didn't do cowardly. Not any more.

Decision made.

I saturated the sheets with relief, melting into the bed, soaking the pillowcase with silent tears. I mourned my old self. My long reign of fuck yous. The broken record of highs and lows. I wept for the youth that should have killed me, the unabashed hunt for pleasure, the search for meaning in pain. It was all over, and I was glad to see it go. I was committed to leaving it all in the past and terrified I wouldn't make it.

But brave bitches do what they have to do.

I got up, showered, took my meds, and walked the halls without looking one way or the other. Just paced my ass over to Elliot's office before his first session.

The door was closed. It was too early, and I had to be out of my freaking mind to try to talk to him in here. Was I trying to ruin his life? Going to see him, telling him I was pregnant, what did I expect? He'd either make too much physical contact or none at all, and we'd both be ripped apart.

*Get it together.*

I didn't want to ruin his life. I had to do this myself. I had to contain both my anxiety and my unreasonable joy. One had to be managed and the other made managing it difficult.

But what about Deacon? He had a right to know as well. In the years we'd been together, we'd never discussed the possibility of children. Would he tell me to get rid of it? I wouldn't if I didn't want to. I didn't need anything from him.

The flip side, of course, was that he might do the less surprising thing and ask for a life with me. I stood on a stone path in the back of the main building and wondered what that would look like. I took the life with Elliot I'd imagined and inserted Deacon. Deacon making eggs. Deacon picking up the kids. Deacon having guests for dinner.

Jesus Christ. No. That wasn't working.

He could be on a ranch in Montana. He could teach the kids to care for the horses and manage the hands. He could teach retribution. Vengeance. Bullies would disappear in the night and be found hanging from the town flagpole in the morning.

I rubbed my eyes.

I didn't need either of them. But I was tied to one for the rest of my life.

A nice long line of flake would really help me get control of this. I laughed at the thought. I was crazy. The last thing I should be doing was snorting. I'd probably damaged the baby forever as it was with Jack's stupid tar shit.

Fuck it. I couldn't talk to either of those guys. Not good for my mental health. What was I supposed to say? *Blah blah pregnant blah blah might be yours might not?* Westonwood was the best place for me.

I was so deep in my thoughts, I wasn't looking where I was going, and I bumped right into Warren. In the sunlight, I could really see him. His tight curls had gotten fuzzy and grown out, and his skin had more grey than pink in it. He must have seen me coming and stood in one place until I ran into him just to see what I'd look like when I recognized him.

"Get the fuck away from me," I said.

"What's with you? Telling people shit? They got everyone on lockdown. Hired half a new staff. You fucked it up for everyone else."

"No, I fucked it up for *you*. You're a fucking psychopath."

"Want to know the best shit about being a psychopath?"

"Fuck you."

"Not caring that other people think you're a psychopath."

"Hey," a voice called from down the path. One of the new security guys. "You two."

Warren and I each took a step backward.

"You all right?" the security guy said to me.

"Yeah."

He stared at Warren until he backed up. My nemesis was apparently losing the war of public opinion in crazyland county. Warren looked into the faces of others to see what he felt about himself, and if he saw something besides admiration, I could only imagine how he'd react.

"Come on, Miss Drazen," the security guard said. He indicated the door back inside. "Your sister's here."

## chapter fifty-one

FIONA

Margie looked shaken to the core.

She didn't, really. She wore a custom-made charcoal grey suit and heels that were just this side of sensible. Her red hair was back in a low twist, and every lash had a reasonable amount of mascara. But her world had been rocked. I knew it as soon as the door closed behind me and she spoke.

"Hello." She hugged me.

I held her for dear life, but it felt as if she leaned into me for support rather than the other way around. She led me to the chair next to her, the same ones we'd sat in the day I was released.

"What's wrong?" I asked.

"I'm here to ask about you. What the fuck happened?"

"I was stupid. That's all. I was trying to get to Warren through his family."

She tilted her head left then right, as if stretching her neck. "It doesn't matter."

"Really?"

"None of it does. Nothing. There's nothing we can do to him or any of them. The rape kit was inconclusive. He's going to walk."

"What did the prosecutor say?"

"Bought and sold. He dropped it. I'm sorry. And we have nothing." She popped open her briefcase. "Our father is on a downward trajectory. The money isn't there. It's tied up. I can't even discuss it. And the Chiltons are waging a PR war to protect Warren's directing career. They put him in the same ward with you, and they're fighting any separation because it makes it look like he's guilty, which he *is*." She slammed her hand on the table. "We have no tools. Not above board. None that play by the rules. And this—"

She put a folder in front of me. Man, she looked like hell.

"I don't know how to make this right for you," she said. "Not yet…"

She stopped herself, sniffing back a sob angrily, and indicated the folder.

I opened it. "Oh."

Irving's pictures faced me. They were works of art. Depictions of a woman in bone-deep pain.

"I made a promise to myself," Margie said. "I'm not relying on the law to protect this family."

"You're a lawyer." I flipped through the pictures. Five. I was in varying stages of pain and nudity. My heart broke for myself.

"Warren is facing consequences," Margie said. "By any means necessary, Fiona."

I turned away from the pictures and looked at her. She had thin damp lines of mascara under her eyes, and her lips were set in a determined line.

"We're making a new name for ourselves. No one fucks with us. When they hear Drazen, they're going to feel nothing but fear. No one's going to hurt you again." She slapped the folder closed. "First thing is stop this from publishing. I'll sneak into Condè Nast and break kneecaps myself if I have to."

My finger traced the outside of the folder, and I set it straight with the edge of the table. "I think we should let it publish."

"They're going to drag you through the mud."

"I don't care. You do what you have to. I…did they tell you?"

"I'm going to assume they didn't."

"I'm pregnant."

I'd seen a cartoon once where the character's face turned to ice, cracked, and fell off in a cute little pile of cubes. Margie's face froze like that, and I waited for the cubes.

"It's not Warren's," I said quickly.

"How do you know?"

Wasn't she there for the rape kit? Didn't she hear my testimony? Maybe not. She wasn't looking right at the affected area for the kit and she'd been out of the room on a call for part of the conversation with the female cop. My god. Did I really have to say this? Was I that brave?

I made myself look casual about it. "He only raped me anally."

Ice cubes to blow torches.

"I'm going to kill him."

"It's fine, I just—"

"Literally. Kill. Then destroy that family."

"I just want to focus on this right now, okay?" I said. "I can't worry about tearing his guts out, which yes, I still want to do. I have to tell the two men who could be the father. I have to stop wanting drugs so bad. I need new friends who don't party. I have to have a life. I don't have the energy for anything else."

She took my hands in hers. "I can't let it go."

"I'm not saying I can either. But it's too much. You figure out the retribution and let me know."

"So you're keeping it? The baby?"

"Yes."

"Daddy's going to shit."

"Fuck him. He'd shit either way."

"That's my girl."

"I need you to get Deacon in here. I don't want to tell him over the phone."

She nodded. "You got it, little sister."

## chapter fifty-two.

ELLIOT

I saw Fiona Tuesday and Thursday in the halls or in the common area. I watched her talk to her brother and a few friends she'd made. We exchanged cordial words. I kept an eye on Warren. I dropped in unexpectedly on the weekend to do paperwork so I could make sure she was all right. I spoke to the staff about keeping her and Warren separated, because even if none of the patients knew about Fiona's accusations, the rest of the world did.

A constant state of stress and emptiness followed me everywhere. I cancelled a session with Lee because I couldn't stand her judgments. She would be right. I had no right to touch a patient, and I didn't care anymore. My right didn't come from a board of ethics. It came from God.

In the hallway right before the staff meeting, I saw her alone. She stood framed in the perspective of the hall, the vanishing point on the horizon. Thirty feet away, she faced me, and as far away as she was, I knew something had changed about her. She didn't buzz. She hummed with the universe in a wordless harmony.

I let my mouth shape a single word without sound. "Soon."

A smile curled one side of her beautiful mouth. She continued to breakfast, and I went to my staff meeting.

"Good morning," I said. Last one there. How long had I been staring at Fiona? I would have to be more careful.

"Chapman," Frances said in greeting, checking my name off the list.

We were all here. Three licensed therapists, two MDs, and three administrators.

"Two incidents this week," Frances said.

I pulled out the reports. One incident involved Chilton. In the other, he was suspected as an instigator. He was indeed using the abundance of rope to hang himself.

"He's acting out," Deanna said. She took his sessions. "The thing with the Drazen girl is upsetting him."

"He's incapable of feeling upset," I said.

"He needs to know his voice is heard in here," Deanna said. "He's being kept away from activities because of an accusation. It's hard on him."

"What's he taking?" Frances pored through his file.

A discussion ensued where they talked about him as if he were a normal person with *feelings* that needed to be managed and a chemical makeup that was like everyone else's.

"What about Paxil?" I interjected. "Get control of the outbursts."

"Contraindicated for suicidal side effects," one of the other therapists interjected.

"In depressed patients," I said.

"Anger is a form of depression," Deanna said.

"Not in his case. He's frustrated. Different."

"I think it's okay," one of the MDs said, not looking up from his agenda.

"Done," Frances said, checking it off her list. "And we're separating him and Fiona. Sorry, Deanna. We'll let them mingle in a week, but the Drazen girl's bound to be emotional and unstable."

"Why?" I asked too fast. I cleared my throat. It didn't look as though anyone had noticed.

"She's pregnant and on med reduction."

Every nerve ending in my body fired a signal to my brain to stop what it was doing. Don't react. Stay still. Look down. Blink. Produce spit. Breathe. Swallow. Fucking breathe.

They moved on to other subjects. I stared at the way my pencil wove through my fingers. I placed it at a forty-five degree angle to the edge of the paper, which was at a ninety-degree angle to the edge of the table.

Blink.

Clear fog from eyes.

Don't think about it.

Pregnant.

Is she keeping it?

Shut up.

Is it mine?

Forget it until you're out of this room.

Does it matter?

I want it. I want it.

We flipped the page, and as I placed my pencil at the exact angle that gave me some measure of aesthetic control, I saw where the tip landed. The visitor list.

*Deacon Bruce. Wednesday. 9am.*

The pencil broke between my fingers.

"I need to come in on Wednesday," I said.

"We're not doing schedule yet," Frances said, tapping the agenda. She addressed the MD. "Now, the Roberts kid. We've seen improvement..."

I held myself together the rest of the meeting. I left after the standard post-meeting discussion, and I went to my office. I had session in fifteen minutes, but my heart was pounding. I was sweating. My face was on fire.

Jesus fucking Christ.

I want to thank you.

But I don't know if I can.

I want it I want it IwantitIwantit.

"God, I hate this." I said to the heavens. "I want to talk to her."

And I couldn't. I couldn't.

Could I?

If I did and lost my license, any good I was doing with anyone would be wiped away. People who needed me on Alondra would be abandoned. Patients in Westonwood I was making progress with would be left with fucking Deanna, who had no talent and too much ambition.

"Can't. Be patient. Jesus, I want to talk to her for five minutes."

The need was physical. Chemical. Every cell in my body pulled toward Fiona. I wanted to tell her I wanted her. Wanted the baby. Wanted us in every way. My insides felt bigger than my outside. Soon, they'd shred me and I'd be nothing but my desire.

My hands were on the arms of the chair, and I looked at the blank space six inches in front of me.

"Get through today. People are counting on you. She's okay. You're okay."

I took a breath and stood. The window looked out on to the garden. Warren walked east with a younger kid at his side. Fiona walked in the opposite direction, alone. I clenched my fists when they passed. Nothing happened. They didn't even look at each other. I released the tension from my fists. I almost turned away in relief until I saw Warren spin around and point at Fiona's back with one hand and grab his crotch with the other. She turned as if sensing something, and he blew her a kiss with his hand still on his junk. She walked away.

*Keep her away from that animal.*

The edict came clothed in my father's voice, and I never disobeyed my father.

chapter fifty-three.

FIONA

I started hating the word "pregnant." The juiciness of it. The way it stuck in the mouth. The weight of the shame I was supposed to feel and didn't. The silence I knew I'd hear after I said it.

I couldn't sleep Tuesday night. I heard every bump and thump. My room was on the top floor, and at one point during the night, it sounded as if someone was doing the tango on the roof. The crickets outside were extra loud, their song unimpeded by the thick glass. The squeak and splash of a mopping bucket came from the hall around midnight.

Then silence.

I listened to the sound of my heartbeat. My breaths. Felt every inch of my body against the sheets and clothes. The air had weight. It smelled of bleach and oranges. The mint in my mouth was swallowed into the lingering taste of dinner.

I didn't feel sorry for myself. I felt called to do something I hadn't considered in my rush to put things inside my body. I let that purpose fill me in the empty space of the night. Breathed it in. Let it sit. Breathed junk out.

I lost count of how many hours I was awake, or how many breaths I took. Time on the clock wasn't important. Only the lightening of the ceiling as the sun rose mattered.

It was Wednesday. It was the day I took matters into my own hands.

***

Frances opened the door to the conference room, and I held my breath. Deacon walked in. He still took up too much room. Still commanded and demanded without speaking a word. Still looked at me as if I was his and his alone.

"You have half an hour until session," Frances said, looking at Deacon then me. "Do not leave this room."

I nodded. He smiled at her. Her eyes narrowed. She found him attractive, of course. She was human. She left, snapping the door closed.

"Hi," I said in a little girl voice I didn't know I had. Shit. I'd have to buck up.

He sat next to me and scooted his chair so our knees were touching. "Kitten." He took my hands.

"Don't call me that." I couldn't look at him, but his eyes were on me. I knew it by the way my skin reacted.

"You wanted to see me?"

"You were right. I'm not submissive. Not the way I thought. Not the way I thought I needed to be."

"I think that's where a lot of your acting out came from. You can switch. I can teach you."

"Yeah. You could. I know. All that. But I don't think that's going to do it for me. Maybe. I don't have any answers. I want a fresh start. Need one, actually. And I needed to say that before saying what I wanted to see you about. Because I'm not going to be bossed into doing anything. It's my life."

He didn't speak. He just let my words hang between us as I watched how our hands looked together. I was too small for him. Too insignificant. And while that would have scared me before, now it seemed so true it freed me.

I looked at him. He was waiting. He'd put on aftershave and a clean suit so I could tell him this. Better make it good.

"The last time I was here, they removed my IUD, and I was too medicated and fucked in the head to know it." Understanding passed over his expression, and I rushed to fill in the space. "You're going to ask if it's yours—"

"Stop."

He was still a dominant personality, so when he said stop, I stopped.

"I'm asking no such thing."

"I need you to let me go."

He unclasped our hands and leaned back, elbow on the table, finger tapping his lip. "No."

"Deacon, really? What the fuck is it with you?"

"Never." He tapped his finger to make his point. "I'll never. Let. You. Go."

I let out a breath of complete and utter fucking exasperation.

"And let me tell you something." He pointed at me. "I took responsibility for you a long time ago. Now maybe you've moved on. But I don't move on. That's not my way. You are always mine, and anyone who hurts you has me to deal with."

"God, Deacon. Please. Please don't do this."

"I've done a lot wrong with you. I pushed you—"

"I begged for it."

"No." He sliced the air with his hand and spoke firmly. Stating facts. "You were put here, in this place, because of me. I'm going to fix it. I'm making it right for you and my child. Then I'm leaving. Not for me, but for you. There's nothing here for me after that."

"After what, exactly?"

He stood. I stood with him.

"Deacon, after what?"

He grabbed me so fast I didn't have a chance to blink and held my face, crashing his lips onto mine, pushing his tongue into me. I let him do it. I let him kiss me, and I returned it for the years we'd had, for what he taught me, for being by my side after all the wrong I'd done.

I gave him that kiss fully, because it was the last.

The door opened.

"Fiona," Frances said, "that'll be enough of that."

I pulled away, giving Frances an apologetic look. Behind her, Elliot walked down the hall in the opposite direction.

## chapter fifty-four

ELLIOT

I recognized his black Range Rover. Eighty-thousand dollar car. Clean as a whistle. It shone like patent leather and pulled light into it at the same time.

He came out of the building, squinting in the morning sun. He saw me and didn't rush. Didn't slow down or acknowledge me until he was close enough to speak without shouting.

"Doctor." He blooped the car. The locks clicked.

"Mister Bruce."

"I'm not threatened by you. At all." He opened the door to get in.

"I don't expect you to be. But I need to get her things. She's not coming back to you."

He slammed the door shut and came at me. I resisted the urge to step back.

"You let him walk around in the same building with her."

"It's not me."

"You let him continue to exist on the earth. To breathe. And not to better protect her. Not for her interests, but yours. *You* need to keep it secret. *You* need to follow your boss's instructions. *You* need to walk a tightrope, and you put her in danger to do it. If she's incompatible with your career, then you have to choose one. Only cowards want both."

He didn't wait for me to answer. He got in and slammed the door. I got out of the way so he could get by without hitting me, and I watched him go with my hands in my pockets.

He was right.

God damn if he wasn't right.

chapter fifty-five.

FIONA

Initially, I wanted to talk to Elliot to explain what he'd seen, or didn't see. I had no idea, then as I got to the end of the hall, I wondered what Deacon had meant by making it right for me. Who was he threatening exactly?

Was he threatening Elliot?

I picked up the pace. He wasn't supposed to be in on Wednesday, so he had no sessions.

His office door was ajar. I was well aware of what I meant to him while I was in here. I was the end of his career. So I didn't burst in as if I had the right to. I rapped lightly and pushed the door just a little. I wouldn't get him into trouble. We'd keep the door open so we'd be seen across the room from each other or sitting with a desk between us.

The door swung easily into the dark room. The blinds were closed, letting through thin lines in a ruled notebook of light. The desk was still neat. The chair was pushed in. The book-cases were full of the usual thick volumes with acronyms for titles.

I opened the door all the way.

The couch where he'd hypnotized me was where it always was, squat and satisfied in its glory.

Framed diplomas checkerboarding the wall. California Board of Psychology dot-dot-dot squiggle-squiggle. Who had I been then? The same girl? Didn't feel that way. Jumping over that desk to strangle him for suggesting I'd stabbed Deacon was a million years away.

Maybe he'd left for the day. Maybe he'd seen me with Deacon and split. Maybe he'd just gone to Alondra. Maybe Deacon was going after him tonight. Maybe tomorrow. Maybe he'd implied he was going to tear Warren apart and Elliot was safe.

I turned that over in my head on my way to the common area with its soothing video of flowers and fields. I had the group thing in fifteen minutes, and I couldn't talk about anything that was on my mind. Again. I saw someone I knew in the cafeteria, and I got into the food line. The bell for lunch had rung a few minutes before, and my stomach was ready.

"Hey, sexy," came a voice so close to me, I heard it just as I felt the body attached to it. Fucking Warren.

"Get away from me," I hissed and went to a table.

Over his shoulder, I saw Elliot watching us. He didn't look right. I had a second to wonder if he'd seen me with Deacon before Warren opened his stupid mouth again.

"Your brother and I are partying on the roof tonight." He threw himself in a chair two spaces away. Far enough away to say he wasn't touching me. "Wanna come?"

He said "come" with a slither.

Jonathan clapped Warren on the back. "That shit you said? Baby's a liar."

"Always has been," Warren added with a wink, and Jonathan sat between us, slapping down his plates. "So, partying tonight?"

"No way, dude," Jonathan said, all bro-like. "Not going in the pokey again."

They laughed together, and I knew through all of Jonathan's denials, Warren made my brother feel good, as if he was a part of something. Some boy club made especially for the adolescent son with seven sisters. Was this kid ever going to be a man?

I looked between my brother and my rapist, and I knew all had been forgiven. Friends again. Nothing but a little roofie-laced scotch on tap for later.

"Don't do it," I said to Warren.

He just smiled. Behind him, an orderly rushed to us. He was going to pull Warren away from me. I wanted that. I wanted him as far away as possible, but I also wanted him incapacitated for my brother's sake.

I didn't have time to think too deeply about what I was doing, but I wasn't in some thoughtless rage either. I wasn't blinded by firing glands or rushes of emotion. "Jonathan, did I ever tell you what Warren did the day I left? Why I looked kind of off?"

"What?" he asked, poking his fork into his meat.

Warren tilted his head, as if wondering where I was going with this. One eye narrowed. "What *I* did? You mean what *we* did?"

Of course that was the tack he was taking. I didn't have time for his shit. I couldn't allow Warren to meet with Jonathan until I'd told my brother what he was dealing with.

I very coldly stood and pivoted behind my chair. I moved it, feeling its weight. The orderly behind Warren slowed down since it looked as though I was moving away.

I breathed and lifted the chair, quickly calculating how to swing it so it didn't hit Jonathan. There was a scream, a tray clattering. I breathed and brought the chair down on Warren's head. It bobbed, and he tipped off his chair, splayed on the floor.

I grabbed a fork and jumped on him.

In the tunnel vision of violence, I saw that I had enough time to gouge out his eyes. I could see the path of my hands and smell his blood as it splashed on my face. It would feel so good. So good. The last drug I'd ever need.

I raised my arm to make my vision a reality. I could practically smell his psycho fucking blood. Aggression took up most of my brain, leaving no room for logic.

I was pulled away before I even touched him. Furniture clattered and squeaked.

I made a show of resisting, but I had no intention of going anywhere. I called his name. I kicked someone. Got away. Got caught. Flooded with endorphins and adrenaline, I saw Warren being helped up like a victim. A sad, sorry victim who wouldn't hurt a fly, but there was enough blood going down his face to ensure a trip to the infirmary. Maybe an overnight stay.

I felt a pinch in my arm as they shot me with a trank, and my last thought was…as successes went, this wasn't too bad.

## chapter fifty-six

ELLIOT

I wasn't kidding myself into thinking I was Deacon Bruce. The man had a core of quiet violence I would never develop. Whatever he had in his head to do to keep Warren away from Fiona was probably more than I was capable of doing, or getting away with for that matter.

But what I was doing wasn't working.

Once Fiona was subdued and Warren taken to the infirmary, I went to my boss's office and closed the door.

"Doctor," she said dryly.

"You need to do more to separate Fiona Drazen and Warren Chilton."

"I hear. She's really a bag of tricks."

"He was standing close to her, whispering in her ear. She has PTSD from what happened. Her reaction was totally within the norm after what he did."

"Allegedly did."

I put my knuckles on the desk and leaned over it. "He needs to be in a high-security facility. Westonwood runs one in Salton Sea."

"Yeah. No." She pushed her chair back and laced her fingers over her rib cage. She seemed too smug, too relaxed for the conversation. "No criminal conviction, no Salton Sea."

"If you won't do something, I will. This place is a really juicy story for the *Times*. Psychiatric resort for the rich? They'd love to shred you."

"You don't give a damn about your job at all, do you?"

"No. I don't."

"All this for a patient? A single patient?" She raised an eyebrow, tapped her finger against the top of her hand.

"Every patient counts."

"Tell me something. Everyone else is fine with how we're handling it. Why are you throwing yourself in front of this?"

"Am I the only one who cares?"

"In what way?" She crossed her legs. She was waiting for me to admit the whole thing. Frances was wasting her time as an administrator. Given the right circumstances, she could crack a man open with her posture from ten feet away.

"I don't think it matters," I said.

But it did. Betrayal mattered. I was denying Fiona three times before the cock crowed. Frances would question me as long as I'd let her, and I'd continue to say she was just a patient until the very edges of my soul were blunted into the shape of renunciation.

"Say it, Chapman. I'm getting bored."

"I'm in love with her. And you can save me the countertransference speech."

She leaned forward. "I wouldn't waste my time."

She swung her computer screen around. *You* magazine's website had posted a picture of Fiona and I talking over buttercups in a Koreatown coffee shop. In it, I held her hands as I told her it was all going to be all right.

"I just wanted to hear you admit it," she said. "But what we have going on here is enough to lose your license over. From what I can see, this was what you wanted the whole time. So congratulations."

"You need to separate them."

"Or what? You're going to tell everyone? With your credibility shot to hell? Now you're just a disgruntled ex-employee. I'll let you go to your office and pack up while I inform the board."

She turned her computer back and typed. I backed toward the door. I had a lot to say, but no patience for the answer.

"You know," she said, "when I was at Loyola, they had a date rape problem they didn't talk about." She glanced at me long enough to say, "Jesuits," then went back to the screen. "Big secrecy game. Like the Opus Dei, those guys. And it didn't occur to me that someone I went on a date with wouldn't get the signals for no—like a struggle or biting. I mean I liked the guy. Right? We're in my parents' basement and I'm trying to rationalize two things. I liked this guy on one hand. On the other, he's hurting me. Even during it, I made excuses for him like, 'He's choking me, so I *can't* say no,' and 'Maybe I should have said it louder when he started, but I was afraid my parents would hear because he wouldn't...'" She stopped typing, sniffed, cleared her throat. "Just *do that.* Right? I must be mistaken somehow. And when I went to the school clinic the next day, you know what they said?" She made eye contact as if she expected an answer but kept talking before I could give one. "They said, 'You'll get over it, Frances. But he's a shining star. It wouldn't be fair to ruin his life over this. One. Incident.'"

I let the story hang there for a moment, fermenting in the sour air between us.

"I'm sorry." I had an arsenal of right things to say in that situation. It was part of my training. But she knew my weapons of compassion better than I did.

She cleared her throat again and opened her drawer. "I always leave these on the desk." She tossed a ring of keys in front of me. "Anyone can grab them. I'm told it's going to get me in trouble one day."

She went back to her work. Was this a trap? The story, the keys, the pantomime of looking away?

"I'm glad you love her," she said. "You both need it. Now get out of here."

She must have hit a button or something, because the door opened behind me. Bernie, the orderly, put his hand on my shoulder. I quietly took the keys and let myself get hauled away without thanking her.

***

I had a couple of boxes of things I'd managed to grab with security's supervision. None of my files on my patients came with me. Books, diplomas, a few knickknacks.

I pulled over a mile outside the facility, while still in the quiet wilds of Palos Verdes, and took a deep breath.

Well, that was fun.

I'd associated losing everything for Fiona with loud noises and some kind of physical pain. I'd accepted it. Knowing better did nothing to reduce my mind's commitment to the image of a hammer coming down, being hurled off a cliff, breaking bones, and a shame so all-encompassing that strangers would see it a block away. My left brain I knew that if I lost everything, I wouldn't cease to exist. But I couldn't imagine anything after it, and the fear had come from the black hole I'd be sucked into afterward.

Elliot Chapman was here a minute ago. Now he isn't anywhere.

But I was breathing. I was sitting in my car with a normal heart rate. The birds were singing, the leaves rustling, and the world was turning the way it always did.

I wasn't afraid for my existence at all.

I was afraid for Fiona. She was stuck in a ward with a vengeful psychopath, and no one was watching him. I should have done something already. I should have taken care of this instead of trying to stay on the narrow path.

Well, I'd been thrown off the path into the black hole I feared.

I weighed the keys in my palm. There were about thirty, and they all looked the same.

How far was I willing to go?

The sensible thing to do was drive away, leave California, try to get a license in another state. Not get attached. Not fall in love with a patient again. Not stick my head out from behind my defenses. Any normal person would lick their wounds and slink away.

Love wasn't worth it. All the psy journals said so.

Well, the theological journals said love was always worth it. And my experience of listening to people talk about their relationships said otherwise.

*He stole his brother's girlfriend because he couldn't live without her.*

*She betrayed her husband because she fell for another man.*

*They broke the law to defy parents who stood between them.*

*He stayed by her through her manic phase.*

*Poverty.*

*Pain.*

*Sickness.*

*Death.*

I'd heard love transcend all of it and never believed it. Not until she came. Fiona put it all into place for me. She made all the stories make sense. All the reckless, senseless, bold, beautiful, risky, irresponsible, brutal, and selfless acts I'd heard about but never understood came into focus through the lens of love.

This was past wanting her. Past possessing her. Past fucking her or protecting her.

How far was I willing to go?

I was willing to be self-destructive, negligent, brave, audacious, and stronger than I ever believed possible.

But I wasn't willing to be stupid. Intentional failure wasn't acceptable, so there was a bigger question.

How far was I *able* to go?

I let the weight of the keys pull my hand down, and I closed my fingers around them.

Nothing to lose really. Except her crazy ass.

I slipped my phone from my pocket and found the numbers I needed, took a deep breath, and dialed the first.

chapter fifty-seven.

FIONA

The quiet woke me. Isolation. I opened my eyes. It was neither dark nor light. Every corner and ridge was equally lit
in a flat, colorless white. That meant it was nighttime. During
the day, it was brighter so your circadian rhythms didn't get
cocked up.

They'd put me in a straitjacket even though I hadn't been
resisting.

"Fuckers," I whispered but didn't mean it. Not really.

I shouldn't have been surprised. This was what they did.
This was the good news. I didn't know why I hadn't thought of
it sooner. Now they'd separate us like they meant it.

I just laid there looking at the little camera eye in the center of the ceiling.

No one came. I couldn't have been in too long. My arms
didn't ache, and I wasn't hungry. I didn't have to pee or anything, but hours went by in my mind. I listened for Elliot's
voice in my cells, the smooth one he used for hypnosis. The
one that suggested strongly. The exact opposite of Deacon's
Dominant voice, which commanded as if he had already been

obeyed. Two sides of the same coin, those voices and the men who breathed them.

I closed my eyes and touched Elliot's body, tracing every bone from toe to head with my fingertips. He had Deacon's face, with its stark blue eyes and unforgiving jawline. And they melded together into one man I'd hurt irrevocably with my selfishness and immaturity.

"God," I whispered, "I know you're there. I don't want to mess up anymore. I don't want to be a fuckup. It's hard. Too hard. And it hurts everyone. I can't live like this. I'm tired of being alone. Alone and thinking no one understands. Elliot says you don't make deals, so I'm not going to make a deal. I'm just going to say, I see you there, and when I'm about to fuck up, I'm going to think of you and do better."

I said that prayer over and over, changing it slightly, repeating words until they flowed and it became my breath.

Change. My way of thinking, my way of speaking, walking, breathing. I was going to believe I could change until everyone else did. In my bones, I knew the higher power I was talking to existed, and it believed in me.

## chapter fifty-eight

FIONA

They'd moved me to a proper isolation room with a bed and toilet. I was there for three days. Frances came to talk to me about Warren, and I told her clearly and intelligently why I'd hit him with a chair. She nodded and didn't say much. A new therapist named Sol came in to say hello. I was back to private sessions when I got out, and not with Elliot.

Probably for the best.

I got the sense that things were happening outside the door, but I didn't ask about them. I just asked myself what I was going to do with my life when I was out.

I was good at partying, being seen partying, and making other people want to be me. I didn't know if that was something I should spend the rest of my life doing. Not with a baby coming. I'd never cared if I was terrible at everything I tried, but being bad at motherhood wasn't an option. I couldn't fail. That wasn't allowed.

When they opened the door and walked me to Sol's office, I'd come no closer to a solution to the problem.

Sol indicated the chair across from his desk, and I sat. He was almost completely bald, portly, with thick glasses. His wedding ring squeezed his finger, and I wondered if he could get it off if he tried.

"Miss Drazen," he said with a slight New York accent, "nice to see you again."

"Nice to be out."

"I bet. Do you want to tell me how you're feeling?"

"Sure. I'm, uh. I have this headache from being inside too much, and my joints feel kind of numb. I want to go for a run or something."

"Do you want something for the headache?"

"No. I'm okay."

He sat back and laced his fingers together over his belly. "I read your file. You're a very interesting young lady."

"Thanks. Not feeling real interesting right now."

"You're what I call a 'truth teller.' A fascinating personality type."

"I've been lying to myself for a long time."

He smirked and nodded then pointed his finger. "That's the root of your suffering, I think. But first, I need to tell you what happened while you were in isolation."

"Is my brother okay?"

The words came out before I even thought about it. He was the only thing I cared about in this mess, and I hadn't even realized it until I asked about him first.

"He's fine." Sol smoothed his pants, brushed something off his knee. "There was an incident on the grounds here."

"Who?" I wasted the question. I knew exactly who it was.

"Warren Chilton. He was found behind the garden where the creek is fenced off."

I knew he was watching my reaction closely, so I tried not to cheer internally. "Found?"

"It's a little gruesome."

"Tell me anyway."

"He was hanging from a tree. He's paralyzed from the neck down."

I blinked back my reaction and failed at hiding my shock. He was alive? Was I relieved or disappointed? Both? Some other third thing that had just released a twist in my gut I'd forgotten? "That's too bad. I just wanted to hit him with a chair."

"Really?"

"No. I wanted to break his head with a chair. Or whatever. I wasn't too picky about what I broke. Wow," I said, realizing he was alive and his dick wouldn't work. I almost laughed and cried at the same time, but ended up doing neither.

He nodded. "Wow is right. I know you and he have a history. You're going to hear a lot of rumors in the rec room. The police are taking this very seriously."

"I'll do a little truth telling." I shrugged. "I'm glad I was in isolation, because I wanted to do much worse to him."

"I'm glad you were in isolation too. This way, we can turn this lying to yourself around and get you out of here without interference. You ready for that?"

"Yes. Yes, I am."

"Good. I'm approving you to be deposed by the LAPD, and we'll get to work first thing tomorrow. You'll still have group starting this afternoon."

I stood, ready to take it all on.

## chapter fifty-nine

FIONA

The cops asked me how much I hated Warren, and I didn't hold back. They couldn't put me away for hating the motherfucker, and apparently I wasn't the only one. They asked about Deacon. I told them he was in Eritrea as far as I knew. They asked about Elliot. I told them to ask Elliot about Elliot. I hadn't spoken to him since I was back in Westonwood. They asked if Warren had been suicidal and if he'd been into breath play or asphyxiation with me, as if he and I were "into" anything together.

They let me go with a warning that they might ask more later. It was lunchtime, and all I wanted to do was run to Jonathan. When I saw him down the hall. I broke into a gallop and jumped into his arms.

"I heard," I said into his shoulder.

"You don't know half of it," he said into my ear then dropped me. "It's good to see you. Really good." He shook his head.

"Are you all right?"

He put his arm around me and guided me through the food line then to a small table where Karen sat alone. I kissed her cheek and sat. She had a plate in front of her with slices of cantaloupe. Jonathan dropped into the chair across from me.

"Do you have to eat that here?" she asked Jonathan, pointing at his steaming plate of protein with her fork. "It smells disgusting."

In answer, he speared a slab of meat and potato and shoved it into his mouth. Karen sighed and dropped her eyes to her plate. She cut the tiniest sliver of melon with a steak knife and put it in her mouth without letting the tines touch her lips.

"How is it?" I asked.

"Not bad."

I looked at Jonathan then back at her.

"You're eating," I said.

"Don't make a big deal about it, or she'll stop," Jonathan said around a mouthful of lunch.

"Okay." I poked at my plate. "It's good to see you guys. Good to be out."

"Now that he's gone," Karen said softly, "it's better in here. Like I can breathe and think at the same time."

I nodded. We ate in silence, air heavy with all the things I wanted to know. I kept glancing at my brother and my friend.

"I noticed the cracks in the ceiling for the first time last night because I wasn't sleeping in a ball." Karen swallowed a paper-thin sliver of melon as if she were swallowing an entire beefsteak tomato. "I thought, wouldn't it be cool to have a georgette scarf with those cracks in it? Such a nice print. And then last night, I thought about how Warren was hanging. All twisted and tangled up like he was fighting his way out. That's what they said. It was so complex, and I thought... ropes. A print of ropes on a scarf that when you tied it, the print was straight, but when it was flat, it was like Warren. Twisted."

"That's a plan," I said.

"He was hanging by the throat for three hours and didn't die. Just a broken neck," she said as if continuing the same conversation, glancing at me sidelong. "Because of the way he was snarled."

I swallowed my food with effort. "What else?"

Karen and Jonathan glanced at each other. Jonathan smirked.

"The whole camera system was on the fritz," Jonathan said. "They think Warren did it because he met me on the roof."

"No."

Two letters one syllable for, *Tell me you didn't do it. Tell me he didn't do it to you. Tell me you weren't involved.*

"He was passed out up there," Karen said, tilting her head toward Jonathan.

"Fuck you," he replied then turned back to me. "We had a few drinks."

"I told you not to," I growled.

"I had my reasons."

Three days had gone by, and in my brother's green eyes were another few years of maturity. A few more decades of experience in seventy-two hours.

"What did you do?" I practically spit the question in half whisper, half growl.

"I'm just a stupid kid," he said flatly. "He roofied me." A little smirk touched his lips, and he didn't break my gaze.

"And Nortyl'd himself pretty good," Karen said. "Without that, I don't think he would have tried to commit suicide. Westonwood's in big trouble for leaving that stuff where a patient could get to it."

My gaze didn't leave Jonathan's.

"He didn't try to commit suicide," I said.

"The Nortyl wiped his memory of everything that night but the need to die," Jonathan whispered "die" with a pop, as if pulling the trigger on the word.

He'd fooled me, and maybe everyone. He'd never been Warren's friend. Never believed him, at least not during my second turn in Westonwood. He'd known what Warren did to me—maybe from Margie, maybe from the rumor mill—and had kept it to himself until he could do something about it.

The face I saw over the cafeteria table wasn't sixteen years old. It was a hundred and sixteen.

"You're scaring me," I said.

"I was passed out."

"Alibi notwithstanding, asshole."

"You know what was weird?" Karen said, still intent on the cantaloupe pieces. She was really making a dent in them. "They fixed the holes in the fence after we left. And there were no new ones. The paramedics spent ten minutes looking for keys then just cut their own hole. No one can figure out how he got back there." She scrunched her face up as if she was sick. "Oh. I have to lie down."

"You're not going to puke, are you?"

"No. It'll pass. I just…" She didn't finish but got up and went for the couches, leaving my brother and me alone.

I held up my hand. "Open pledge."

He held up his hand. "Open for yes or no questions."

"You don't get to dictate what you answer."

"I was passed out. I went up for a drink because I was mad at you and I didn't believe you. He gave me mine. He drank his. We had a few laughs. I forget the rest. Cameras went back on an hour later, and I was still there. Passed. Out. Ask the cops. Pledge closed."

"No! You're leaving stuff out!"

He stood and scooped up his tray. "I love you, sister."

The bell for afternoon sessions rang.

I grabbed his arm before he could walk away. "Jonathan. Who got to you?"

"You did, stupid." He kissed my cheek and strode off.

I was supposed to be in group session in five minutes, but all I could do was put the Nortyl and the complex knots together with Jonathan getting Warren out of his room when the cameras were down. Pack that all in a bong and smoke it, and even with the hundred holes in the story, it added up to one thing.

I was loved by a team of smart, shrewd, criminally-inclined vigilantes.

But I was loved.

If I denied that any longer, I was calling them all liars. And if I denied I was worthy of it, I was convincing myself they were delusional and stupid.

I wasn't lying to myself anymore. Not about that.

chapter sixty.

FIONA

Rumors about Warren were vicious and horrifying. I could tell the truth from the lies, because every detail traced back to someone who loved me.

LIE: Warren was practicing autoerotic asphyxiation.

TRUTH: The knots were so tight they broke skin.

LIE: Warren had been given Nortyl for bipolar disorder.

TRUTH: The rope he'd been tied with wasn't from anywhere inside the institution.

Bottom line: Warren had been in a state of soul-ripping, mind-blunting pain when he broke his neck, and he woke up dickless. That was all I needed to know.

I didn't try to get out. Didn't strategize the right things to say or do. No tricks. No games. Without Warren around, a calm fell over crazytown. No one was taking off-script drugs or paying for favors in blow jobs. Mark got let go a week after Warren was wheeled away, and couple of guys in security were let go quietly. A PA confessed to getting him pills but swore he never doled out Nortyl. No one believed him.

Sol stayed around. Deanna stayed. There was a rumor Frances had to fight for her job. Elliot was gone.

I knew he was waiting. I told Sol I had someone. He was from outside my world. He was loyal and decent. He set the right path by example, not force, and he loved me. Crazy as it was, he loved me. Of all the world's gifts, that was the greatest, and I wasn't going to decide I didn't deserve it. Only he could decide that, and if he said I was good enough for him, I wouldn't argue otherwise.

Except when I did. Old habits died hard, but they died.

"Your brother's getting out in a week," Sol said from behind his desk.

"I want to to wait for him."

"That can be arranged. Why?"

"I want to walk him out. And this way we can share a ride."

"I didn't know carpooling was so important to you."

"There are ten of us. Think about it. The Drazen Carpool can probably wean the US off foreign oil."

He shifted forward. "Besides running the biggest carpooling organization in the country, what are your plans when you leave here?"

"Get lunch?"

He cleared his throat, which was code for, "I get the joke now answer the question."

I looked out the window. The sky was a flat blue. A black speck of a bird shot across it and was gone. "I think I need help. Deanna talks about meetings. I know the ones in Hollywood. Big celebrities go, and they're not treated any different. No one notices." I brushed the velvet pile on the chair until it was all the lightest color. "I need new friends anyway. The ones I have are nuts."

"You might need a job."

I laughed. Right. I'd been cut out of Drazen money like an infection. "Yeah. I don't know. I can sell the condo and a car and invest in something."

"Such as?"

"I know a guy who makes excellent designer drugs."

"Fiona," he scolded.

"I'm joking." I joked because I didn't have an answer. I didn't know what I wanted to do, but I wanted him to know I was thinking about it. I took my life seriously, even if I didn't have the answers. So I riffed on a pebble of a notion Karen had left for me. "Maybe something with scarves and clever prints." I moved my hands around as if spooling an idea around them. "I don't think making stuff is my thing, but I'm good at people. People who make stuff. Like that. And I can wear the scarves out to parties. Calmer parties. The ones people with babies go to. Be seen. Get photographed. You know, that-do-that-I-do."

"It's a start," he said. "Risky, but I guess your family won't let you starve."

I laughed. I thought of Karen, how she wouldn't starve if she had something about herself to love.

Maybe this wasn't a bad idea.

## chapter sixty-one

ELLIOT

I got to the Westonwood parking lot before Margie Drazen. We had a cup-of-tea bet going on about whether she'd make it first from Beverly Hills or I'd make it from Torrance. I cheated and left twenty minutes earlier than I said I would. She pulled in right behind me.

"What time did you leave?" she asked as she walked from her Mercedes toward my shit Honda. She had tall paper cups in each hand.

"Seven ten." Admitting it made me a lousy cheater.

"You beat me fair and square." She handed me a cup.

"We were starting at seven thirty."

"I left at seven."

"See you in hell." I took a sip of my tea.

I'd just gotten done with an overnight at Chino State, where I usually waited for something to happen then felt grateful when nothing did. On-call crisis counselor was the only job I could get with my license being under review. It had been three months, and another three years could go by before I would be off probation. The board never approved of my relationship with Fiona, but I was clear she was the first and the last, and I wasn't giving her up. They called it "lovesickness," and I had to laugh. I was sick, and they were sick, and everyone who ever touched love was most certainly terminally ill. We all died from this disease of love.

"What color did you decide on for your office?" I asked.

"Green for money."

Margie had left her job and started her own firm. She said she needed freedom to pursue her own interests. Like getting Deacon Bruce on a plane in the middle of the night. Like pressing the license review board in my case. Like delivering a set of keys to the director of a mental institution without being seen. Or aiding Declan Drazen in the expensive backhand dismantling of the Chiltons' business. Bit by bit, movie by movie, relationship by relationship, Margie and Declan were moving the pieces on the chessboard to block, sabotage, and break the family. I didn't have details, only the knowledge it was happening, and the news. Charlie Chilton had lost a huge directing deal in the previous week, and all permits for their half-built house had been rejected.

I pitied them. Their son would never recover. But I was just a man. They were in denial over the danger their son posed to other people, and he'd targeted someone I loved. My compassion had limits.

"They're coming," Margie said, putting her cup on the hood of my car.

Jonathan exited first and held the door open for his sister.

She was as breathtaking as ever.

Her strawberry hair bounced when she walked, her chin tilted upward when she saw us, and her body was the most perfectly fuckable thing to ever grace the earth. When she smiled at me and picked up the pace, I couldn't help myself. I ran to her. She was worth running for. Worth every loss in my life. Worth stepping outside the law. Worth living, dying, and everything in between.

She fell into me, and we became arms and lips and hands. Breath and movement. I tasted her, felt her, understood in the way she moved that she and I were connected, and nothing had changed for her in the months we were separated. Even when she pushed herself against me and I felt the extra curve in her belly, nothing had changed.

"You've never been fucked like I'm going to fuck you," I whispered.

I felt her shudder in my arms. Warm and pliable, sharp and twisted, fuck her was the least of it. I was going to love her brutally and unconditionally.

Forever and ever, amen.

## chapter sixty-two

FIONA

We said our good-byes and hurled ourselves into Elliot's car. He took off down the winding road through Rancho at the speed limit. It was warm, so he wore a button-down shirt and slacks without a jacket. I saw his body move, the way his fingers controlled the wheel, the flicking of the wind in his sandy hair.

He didn't say anything. No small talk. No dirty talk. His ocean eyes stayed on the road.

"You've been working out?" I asked.

"It helps redirect my energies."

I put my hand on his knee. He took his hand off the gear shift and clasped mine.

"We have a lot to talk about," I said.

"Yep."

I had phrased the next part in my head a billion times. I didn't know if I'd bring it up right away, but I didn't expect the car ride to be the best time. The fact that he wasn't looking at me would make it easier.

"I'm going to have a baby."

"If it makes it easier for you, I already knew."

"It does," I said. "I don't have to talk you down from shock."

"How are you feeling, by the way?" He turned to me for a second. "They wouldn't tell me anything, and Margie just said 'fine.'"

"No morning sickness or anything. Just hungry." I cleared my throat. "I did get this test done a couple of weeks ago."

"Yes?" he asked.

"I was worried because I did some partying, and she seems okay."

"She?"

"It's a girl."

He squeezed my hand and smiled. God, this was going to be hard.

"They had to put this needle in, and they tested the DNA also, and here's the thing. I was with you, but also, God I hate this—"

"Fiona—"

"Shut up. It was a transition period. There was no crossover. Once it was you, it was you, and it's not a big deal to me but…" I ran the rest together without punctuation. "But in the time this baby was conceived I was with both of you and if you'd let them get a cheek swab we'd know if it was yours I'm sorry but I don't think it's fair for you not to know."

He laughed.

"What's so funny?'

"You."

"Why?"

"Because you think I give a shit." He glanced at me to check my reaction then looked back at the road. "I will never, ever give you a cheek swab or anything else to prove this baby is or isn't mine. You can leave me tomorrow, and I'll claim that baby girl."

I crossed my arms. "I don't know if I'm relieved or annoyed."

"You don't have to be either."

Then gently, as if turning into his own driveway on any other Tuesday, he turned onto a dirt road, followed until it went left, and stopped.

"Where are we?" I asked.

"Alone."

He fell onto me, lips and tongue on mine. Hands up my shirt, taking skin that hadn't felt a man in too long, he cupped my breast and twisted a nipple that needed it so badly, I groaned and cried out at the same time.

"Right here," he said. "I'm taking you right here."

I didn't know how we did it. The Honda had no room for two adults to become one twisting, curling, half-clothed mass of flesh. But against all the odds, against even the laws of physics and logic, we did.

FIONA

Theresa, for all her pearl-clutching and airs of civilized grace, wound up with a devil. He was as handsome and charming as the devil, too. Dark eyes and hair. Full lips. Bit of a Roman nose but not too much. The eyelashes, a defining feminine feature on most people, actually set off a masculinity so intense he seemed as likely to pour from the wine bottle he held, as break it over someone's head.

"Okay," he said with an Italian accent. "Red then. A chianti."

"I'm fine," I said. "Thank you."

He blinked, apparently incredulous. Behind him, the doors opened onto a guest-filled patio and, beyond that, a flowering olive orchard deep in Temecula.

"You're eating," he said. "You have to—"

"Antonio!" My sister Theresa broke in, wedding dress trailing over the tile floor. Good thing it was a huge kitchen. "She doesn't drink. Get off her case."

Bottle in one hand, glass in the other, he spread his arms as if he was the innocent victim of a foreign culture. *"Perche, no?"*

Theresa plucked the glass and wine from him and kissed him. "Get her some water, would you?"

"*Come vuoi tu, Capo.*" He kissed her back.

A guttural sound of flat disgust came from behind me. I jabbed Amanda in the sternum. She exhibited every single annoying trait of adolescence, but being grossed out by kissing and sex? Not annoying.

I didn't want my daughter to be a sexless wonder. I wanted her to be liberated and enjoy her body, but one less thing to worry about was one less thing to worry about.

"I have water, thank you." I tapped my glass with my spoon and the population of the kitchen joined in.

I'd discovered this old Italian tradition within an hour of arriving. If the guests tapped their glasses, the couple had to kiss. I winked at Amanda, and she rolled her eyes. They were blue. Shocking blue. A blue like I'd seen on a face only once before. She was tall and had jet black hair without a touch of red. I wondered if she was my daughter sometimes, especially when her report cards came in looking like every key on the teacher's computer was broken except the letter A.

In response to the clinking glasses, Antonio and Theresa kissed like the newlyweds they were. He whispered something in her ear, and her knees bent a little. Sexual liberation came late to Theresa, but when it came, it came hard.

"Gross," mumbled Amanda, turning a deep shade of red. "Are you going to let Alex see this?"

Alex was our ten-year-old. A pure-strain ADHD case with a joyful laugh and enthusiasm for just about everything. He had sea-green eyes and bright red hair. Completely unaware of social norms, he pushed between Antonio and Theresa to get to me. They separated, laughing.

"Mom!"

"Can you apologize to Aunt Theresa and Uncle Antonio for pushing them, please?"

He spun around. "Sorry!" Then he turned back to me.

I bent my knees to get on his eye-level. His shirt was already untucked and his jacket was probably under a rock somewhere. He could have survived a week on the hors d'ourves stuck to his tie.

"Uncle Jonathan says he can teach me to pitch, and I'm a lefty, so he said I can prob get on any varsity baseball team in the world if I can pitch, and he'll teach me!"

"All right. You can start after the Thanksgiving break."

"No! Today! He says today is as good a day as any and it's only an hour or something out in the orchard please please please.

"You're wearing your good shoes."

He didn't have time to answer before Jonathan appeared above me with a bag of oranges. He'd grown tall and strong and saved the Drazen empire from insolvency right out of grad school. An insolvency the press attributed to Daddy's non-existent drinking problem. It was easier to say Declan Drazen was a drunk than that he'd spent almost every dime taking down Charlie Chilton. Daddy didn't care if the world thought he was a drunk, as long as they didn't know what he really did.

"So what?" Jonathan said. "It's pitching. He's not going to ruin his shoes."

David, my sister Sheila's twelve-year-old, handed Alex a lefty glove with a ball in it. "Had it in the car."

Alex made a pleasepleaseplease face. I loved the fuck out of that kid. He loved doing things. Sports. Art. Writing. Tag. Dungeons and Dragons. People. Overall, he loved people, and I knew he cared more about spending time with his uncle and cousin than he cared about his curveball.

"Is your wife all right without you?" I asked Jonathan.

His wife, a stunning musician with a smart mouth, was about eight minutes to giving birth, and he doted like a mother hen.

"She's surrounded by half of Naples. I can't even get near her." He slung the bag of oranges over his back. "We'll be over that way." He pointed at some vague place out yonder, toward the setting sun, beyond the tables and people dancing.

The three of them took off without another word from me.

An Italian dance had begun out in the yard, and Theresa was hoisted above the crowd like a lily bouncing on the water.

Amanda sat to the side, all in black, a puss on her face that would freeze oceans.

"She's still sulking?" Elliot's voice came from behind me.

"Yeah."

He touched the back of my neck and ran his finger across my shoulder. He knew the exact right amount of pressure to make me forget everything. "You should let her go," he said.

"I can't discuss this anymore."

"But she and I can." He turned me around so I faced the kitchen. It had emptied out, so there was nothing to distract me from his ocean-green eyes. They'd earned some lines at the edges over the years. He'd gotten more impossibly handsome with age. "So she and I win."

"No, you don't." I smoothed the front placket of his clerical shirt. He'd finally done his discernment for the Episcopal priesthood and gone back to spiritual practice. It had been a long, hard slog. Eight years. But at the end of it, he was a new man.

"How about this?" he said. "If you admit the real reason you don't want her to go to Nambia, we'll make other arrangements for next summer." I was about to say she wouldn't be safe when he held up his finger. "The real reason. You know she's safe with Deacon. He'd burn the entire continent down before anything happened to her."

I bit my lips then told him the real reason, which he was damned well aware of. "He'll see her, and he'll know. And she'll know."

"Know what?"

"She's his."

"She's mine. She's always been mine."

"Can we stop kidding ourselves? Please?"

"I don't care about her DNA. I really don't. I've been her father for fifteen years, and he's been a pen pal. When she wanted to sell Girl Scout cookies, who sat in front of the grocery store all weekend? When she wanted to play basketball, who coached the team? When she got her first period, who ran out to get her supplies? Me. She's mine. And she's going to go there and fall in love with the adventure and worship her Uncle Deacon like everyone else, but she knows she's mine."

"What about him?"

"I wouldn't worry about him." He'd always been so confident about his earned paternity, as if things being unimpeachably right in his world made them right everywhere. He was a believer in truth, and his one overarching truth was always that his family was whomever he claimed.

"How's that?"

"I can take him in a fight." He put his arms around me and put his lips to my forehead. "For my family, I'll take him and a hundred like him."

"Men," I grumbled, putting my head on his chest. "Wait. I won the bet. Now that I admitted the real reason, she can go to Monterey next summer."

"You don't want her to, now that you've said the truth out loud."

He was right as usual. Voicing my fear had taken the power from it. Amanda craved adventure and travel. I couldn't hold her back much longer.

"What did I ever do to deserve you?" I asked.

"You let me love you."

"Is that all?"

"Yes."

I turned my back to him, and he wrapped his arms around me, burying his lips in my neck.

"Worth it," I said.

Out on the flagstones, Antonio and Theresa danced. He held her, and when he looked up, our eyes met. He said something to Theresa and she protested, but he pushed her away and bounded up the steps cd through the crowd to the sliding kitchen doors.

"You don't drink wine?" he asked through the screen, as if being dry at a wedding was an impossible concept.

"Sixteen years sober, Antonio. You didn't notice? I've known you six months already."

"Do you have any fun at all?"

"Yes," Elliot answered. "That's my wife's job."

Antonio cocked his head.

"I'm seen having fun," I said. "Didn't Theresa tell you anything?"

"I didn't understand it, I admit."

Elliot let me go, leaving a hand on my neck.

"I find designers. I invest in them. I take them out. People talk. We build a business."

I couldn't tell if he was impressed or doubtful anyone could make money doing something so silly.

"Do you dance?" he asked.

I had to think for a minute. It had been a while. "Yes, as a matter of fact, I do dance."

Antonio slapped open the screen door and addressed Elliot. "I will never get used to a priest having a wife. But, do you mind if yours dances with me?"

"Not at all." He took his hand off my neck. "Be careful with her. She's the most valuable thing I have."

"I will treat her like a precious flower," Antonio said when I took his arm. "But she may have to hold me up. I've had too much wine."

Antonio walked me out to the clearing where a crowd danced under the setting sun. At the edge of the orchard I could see Jonathan kneel next to my son to show him how to hold a baseball, and my nephew pitched oranges against a tree trunk. To my right my daughter pouted because I hadn't told her that yes, she could go to Africa next summer, and behind me, Elliot watched as I danced with my brother in-law. My sister danced in her wedding gown. Margie spoke urgently to my parents. My brother's wife waddled to the bathroom.

We were connected. All of us. By the gestures of our hands and the tones of our voices. By our intentions, our actions, our loyalties, By our willingness to sacrifice for one another, we were joined by the ropes of our love and held fast by the knots of our hearts.

I was among my people, and I was worthy of them.

*Thank you for reading.*


My Goodreads fan group is called CD Canaries: join the group!

Facebook fan-run group, go to http://on.fb.me/18V33wl. Most fun, guaranteed.

Facebook fan page is www.facebook.com/CDReiss.writer. I run this, and it's for official news and announcements.

I'm on Pinterest, Tumblr, Twitter and Instagram with varying degrees of frequency.

My email is cdreiss.writer@gmail.com.

# Acknowledgements

I cannot describe to you how difficult I am to work with. I do everything by the seat of my pants and every person here not only understand and tolerates that, they make it their business to do their jobs under the worst circumstances (that worst circumstance being...me).

Angela Marshall Smith, Cassie Cox for editing the hell out of this thing when it was a mess, thank you.

Erik, my formatter is the balls. He actually pokes me and asks me if I'm done yet, then, after I act like he woke me from a deep sleep, turns around on a dime and hands me something perfect.

Sarah – thank you for the original covers. They were amazing and I loved them. I'm sorry about prudes.

My Canaries and Goddesses, Tony, Diana, Dana, Kaylee, Jean, for tolerating weeks of silence while I finished, thank you.

Christy, I can get on the Dash Wallace website now I swear.

My friends at Fab Four, Kristy, Laura, Lauren, BGP, and the Erotica Consortium keep me together. It's beautiful to have such a support system. I don't know how anyone works without it.

A certain group at a certain company who cut me off promotions because I put a book where you didn't want it, thank you. By keeping it "not personal" but singling me out, you tacitly gave me permission to do this with other books and make money without guilt.

I saved my fans for last. I've thanked you guys a hundred times for this and I'll thank you a hundred more. You waited a long time for Fiona, and never complained while I did other things. I don't know any other writer who has had such a long wait and never got a nastygram. You are the cream of the crop.

Stick around for *Kinky Sexy Dirty*.

[1] She just got out of Westonwood, where she was raped anally by Warren Chilton an hour before release. Her sister, Margie came to get her and Elliot met her at the door, but she decided to go with Deacon because he felt safest after what just happened.
[2] This is what Elliot asked her to do in Use — to be the first catalyst to changing who she was by changing the way she spoke to herself.
[3] Maundy Street is where Fiona lived with Deacon. Number two was the private BDSM club.
[4] These are the words Elliot said at the door as she was leaving Westonwood.

www.ingramcontent.com/pod-product-compliance
Lightning Source LLC
Chambersburg PA
CBHW061524210726
48287CB00006B/1824